Swan Song of A. J. Wentworth

I have had some surprises in my life, not counting the time I was accused of attacking a boy with a cutlass during the after-lunch rest period, but I have rarely been more astonished than when the Headmaster stopped me on my way down the school corridor to take IIIA in Algebra and asked me whether I would like to go to America. I was already a couple of minutes late owing to a trivial mishap in the Common Room and not really in the mood for aimless conversation.

'Generous as is the scale of pay for assistant masters,' I began, trying to keep any trace of irony out of my voice, 'it still does not permit . . .'

'Your gown is on inside out,' he said.

Also available in Arrow by H. F. Ellis

A. J. Wentworth B.A.

H. F. Ellis

Swan Song of A. J. Wentworth

Arrow Books

Arrow Books Limited
17–21 Conway Street, London W1P 6JD

An imprint of the Hutchinson Publishing Group

London Melbourne Sydney Auckland
Johannesburg and agencies throughout
the world

First published by Arrow 1982

None of the material in this book has been collected previously in book form. Half a dozen of the Burgrove episodes originally appeared in *Punch*.

Set in Baskerville by
Rowland Phototypesetting Ltd
Bury St Edmunds, Suffolk.
Made and printed in Great Britain
by The Anchor Press Ltd
Tiptree, Essex

ISBN 0 09 929 1606

Contents

Introduction

Well aware that Mr A. J. Wentworth had indeed returned to Burgrove Preparatory School for Boys for that 'one more term' of which he spoke at the end of his last volume of reminiscences, and furthermore that his final fling (if he will forgive the rather extravagant word) as a schoolmaster included a brief but broadening visit to the United States, I have on a number of occasions asked him – pestered would not be too strong a term – for some account of this well-deserved climax to his long career.

'It was all a long time ago, dear boy,' he is wont to say. 'The world has changed. Back in the sixties – the calendar sixties *and* mine, eheu! and mine – there was a, how shall I put it? A spirit of what d'ye call it that can no longer I fear, I greatly fear, be – in short, I should be misunderstood. My attitude to life and, if I may so express it, my vision of – of things in general is out of fashion. Gone. Gone!'

All the more reason to preserve some record of that vision, I have told him. And now at last, with some reluctance, he has consented to hand over to me the usual mass of diary extracts, jottings on the backs of old envelopes, menu cards and miscellanea, including a snapshot of himself apparently holding up the Empire State Building with one hand (which I have *not* reproduced) and a torn cutting from the *Fenport Chronicle* (which I have). From these documents I have put together as coherent a story as may be of Mr Wentworth's final appearance on the scholastic scene.

The title *Swan Song* is in some ways, perhaps, inappropriate. 'A. J.' is, at the time of writing, neither dead nor dying; nor has he been, throughout the rest of his life, altogether mute.

H. F. Ellis

Kingston St Mary, Somerset 1982

Last Term at Burgrove

Once More into the Breach

So it is to be back in harness again, in Thompson's shoes – metaphorically speaking, naturally, though *gown* might be a better word in the circumstances – since the poor fellow is still making only slow progress it seems. One man's meat is another man's poison, as the saying goes, or the other way round, rather, in this case, because the extra money, such as it is, will not come amiss, especially as Elm Cottage is to be let while I am away, which will be a little more grist to the mill despite the awkwardness as between friends.

I have Miss Stephens to thank for the arrangement, actually, because as soon as she heard that I was to have one more term at Burgrove – and it isn't long before everybody knows my business here in Fenport, I need hardly say – she began to put her irons in the fire and the first I knew about it there she was, calling out to me right across Mellish the chemist's, where I was buying razor blades as it happens. 'Back to the grindstone, then, Mr Wentworth? Back to the grindstone?' she cried, in her jovial way.

'One does not have to sharpen these modern safety blades, Miss Stephens,' I said, to turn it off, and I gave a warning shake of the head, as much as to say that this was neither the time nor the place. But a hint is as useless as a wink to Miss Stephens, as I might have known.

'Oh come, Mr Wentworth!' she said gaily. 'I know all about it. You can have no secrets from *me*.'

'Nor from anyone else, it seems,' I remarked, with a frowning glance at the man Odding, who is always about when not wanted, entitled though he is, I suppose, to buy a tube of what looked like analgesic balsam for his wife. She has trouble with her back, so I hear.

'The thing is,' Miss Stephens went on, quite undeterred, 'that I happen to know of somebody who would just love to spend a month or two in Fenport and is looking for a cottage to rent at the time you will be away. And who do you think,' she added, with what I suppose I must describe as a twinkle, 'that somebody could be? Your old inamorata, Myra Fitch!'

'Really, Miss Stephens!' I exclaimed. 'You have no right – it isn't as if – Myra Fitch, eh? God bless my soul!'

The man Odding was taking a devil of a time paying for his confounded balsam and I hardly knew where to look. 'I don't know I'm sure,' I said. 'I am told it is sometimes difficult to get people out of your house, once you have let them in. Isn't that so?'

'Oh, but you might not want to get her out, Mr Wentworth,' she said, deliberately defeating my attempt to strike an impersonal note. 'Surely Elm Cottage is big enough for two?'

Well, really! I am old-fashioned enough to think that a lady's name should not be bandied about in chemists' shops, however well-intentioned. I did what I could to repair the damage, raising my voice for Odding's benefit and replying with a casual air, 'If this Mrs – I am afraid I did not quite catch the name – if she cares to make me an offer I will certainly consider it,' and with a brusque 'Good day to you, Miss Stephens, and thank you,' was making my way out of the shop when Mellish reminded me that I had forgotten to pay for my blades, which was true, and small wonder, all things considered. The delay enabled Miss Stephens to come close up and prod me in the waistcoat, or pullover actually – an attention I have never relished – and say in a stage whisper, 'It's hardly for *her* to make the offer. That's only for Queens and Leap Years, surely?'

This wilful misunderstanding of my previous remark put the cap on it, and I strode home in no very equitable frame of mind. She means well, but there is a time and place for everything, and not even that in every case. At least, I could not help thinking, I shall soon be safely back at Burgrove where a man's private affairs *are* private. With luck, of course. Gilbert, now I come to think of it, made a jocular remark towards the end of last term which seemed to imply – however, one must hope for the best, as I always do.

Anyway, it is all settled now, and I am glad to know that my few poor possessions will be well looked after by a lady for whom I have a great deal of – well, respect, to put it no higher. Which, I like to believe, is in some degree returned. I shall leave her notes, instructions and so on, about this and that. The gate-leg table, for instance, is more stable with the front flap *down*. Mrs Bretton, I hope, will continue to cook lunch and so on, except on Sundays, and can tell Mrs Fitch about anything I might scruple to jot down. The smallest room upstairs has its difficult moods, though I dare say a pinned-up 'Pull *twice*' note would avoid any embarrassment. One has to think of these things, naturally.

Which reminds me that I must warn our good vicar, Somers, that he will have to find a substitute sidesman to take over my duties at St Martin's (1st and 3rd Sundays, 11 a.m.) during my absence. It is a pity, really. It is only recently that I consented to take on the responsibility, after poor Twitcher (curious name) put rum in one of the vessels and had to be relieved – 'nervous breakdown' they called it but *I* believe it was straightforward revenge for that row over the goats in the churchyard. I was reminded of that time when Blenkinsop (not his real name, of course; one has no wish to tarnish his memory) filled the School Swimming Cup with stale buns and caused a regular upset at Prize Giving. Back, oh, in the thirties, that must have been. *He* wasn't nervous. Just not cut out to be a schoolmaster and hated the whole place from the word go. There was an occasion when even I, as a very young man – but we have all sown our wild oats in our time (wild *goats* in Twitcher's case, what?) and there is no need to bring them up now. I was saying that it's a pity to be handing over my sidesmanship just when I was getting the hang of it. Not, I mean to say, that the simple duties present any problems to a man of my experience. Indeed, I could not help a bit of a chuckle when the vicar began to explain about handing out the hymn books and so on, as if there were some kind of mystique about the business.

'My dear vicar,' I told him, 'I suppose I have handed out at least as many books of one kind or another, not to mention a great many other things, such as nibs, blotting paper and pretty well anything you care to mention, as any man in this parish. It is quite a different kettle of fish, let me tell you, when you have a crowd of young boys clamouring round you rather than a few elderly –'

'Yes, yes, yes, Wentworth,' he interrupted in that tiresome way he has. 'It is worth remembering, nonetheless, that old Miss Salthouse prefers the *large*-print hymn book, and when it comes to the collection –'

'Don't tell me that old Miss Salthouse,' I couldn't resist saying, 'has to have a *large* bag to put her offering in.' It was meant as a joke, of course, but I fear that old Somers, as I discovered at that Vicarage Christmas Party, is not very quick in the uptake. To humour him, I listened with a good grace to the rest of what he had to say, which was little enough in all conscience, and it was certainly no fault of mine that the key of the church safe happened to slip through a grating in the vestry floor, a misfortune against the possibility of which I had emphatically *not* been warned. Accidents never come singly in any case, as I pointed out at the time, referring to an earlier incident too trivial to be worth setting down here. 'No, they always come in threes, I believe,' said the vicar, 'so I'll be off before you can – anyway I must be off.' And off he went, only to trip up over a vase of dead flowers which I had carefully moved out of people's way, thus lending support to the old adage, much to my amusement I need hardly say.

Still, all that is past history now, and here I am once more in the old familiar surroundings. 'Eager for the fray, A. J.?' Gilbert called out as I strolled into the Common Room, and I let it pass with a smile and a friendly nod, not wishing to spoil a rather emotional moment. Fray indeed! He should speak for himself, if that is the way he regards the privilege of trying to knock a bit of sense into a bunch of thick-headed youngsters.

'What's new?' I asked.

'Not this carpet anyway,' observed Rawlinson, hauling himself up from the only decent chair to give me a punch in the ribs by way of greeting. 'And talking of news, what about yours? When is it to be?'

'When is what to be?' I asked, in surprise.

'If A.J. = M.F., what, algebraically speaking,' Gilbert said, 'is the result likely to be?'

'Twins,' said Rawlinson.

'Suffering snakes!' I exploded, for I was determined to show them that I wanted no more of this impertinence. 'Leave my private affairs alone and at least allow me to arrange my books in peace.'

'Quite right, quite right,' said Gilbert. 'The School must come first, Wentworth.'

And so it must, for a matter of twelve weeks or so at any rate. After that, we shall see what we shall see. In the meantime, 'Sorry, old boy!' said Rawlinson, and we all had a glass of sherry out of the cupboard.

A Useful Digression

'Sir, there's one thing I don't quite understand, sir –'

'Indeed, Potter?' I said, throwing a look over my spectacles at the rest of my IIIA boys. 'Perhaps it is just as well. Omniscience is an uncomfortable possession.'

'I mean about wheels, sir.'

I was not aware that we were discussing wheels at the time. Still, the boy had a look of genuine interest, which is something I am always loth to discourage. 'What is the difficulty about wheels, Potter?' I asked.

'Well, sir, I was looking at that circle you've drawn, and I suddenly sort of wondered what would happen if it started rolling –'

'It would fall off the board, you chump,' said Mason.

'What I mean is,' Potter went on, after saving me the trouble by telling Mason to shut up, 'it would roll on its rim, wouldn't it, so when it had gone right round once it would have got as far as it's outside is long, surely?'

'It would have travelled a distance equal to its own circumference, yes,' I agreed.

'Yes. Only – look, sir, would you mind putting an X or something on one of those spokes?'

'Radii,' I corrected, marking a point X about halfway between centre and circumference. 'Well, Potter?'

'Well, sir, when the circumference, when that point A at the end of the radius has gone right round once, X has only gone round once too, only it goes round a much smaller circle, you see, so it ought to get left behind. I mean,' he explained, putting on the extraordinary expression boys use when they are really trying to *think*, 'it can't have gone as *far*.'

'Exactly,' I said. 'Potter has raised a very good point here. Obviously, since wheels do not come in half every time they rotate, there must be a simple explanation of his difficulty. Can any boy tell me what it is?'

'I had a pennyfarthing bicycle once,' Notting shouted. 'At least, anyway, it belonged to another person –'

'So what?' interrupted Wrigley. 'I knew a man who kept rabbits.'

'They have a big circle and a little circle going round together, that's what. So it's the same thing, isn't it, sir?'

'Not quite, I'm afraid,' I said, smiling to smooth over his disappointment. 'The two wheels are not –. What are you doing with those protractors, Mason?'

Mason said that he was explaining to Potter how, when people walked, their feet went much further than the top of their legs at every stride. 'Only their hip joints never get left behind, you see, sir,' he ended, amid general laughter.

'I am much obliged for your assistance, Mason,' I told him. 'But I think perhaps we shall get along faster if you leave the explanation to me. Yes, Henderson?'

'I'm sorry, sir, only I thought you asked *us* if we could explain it.'

'By all means go ahead, if you have a sensible suggestion to offer,' I said, though without a great deal of hope.

'I don't know whether it's sensible or not,' he began, with that tiresome air, so typical of boys of his age, of abjuring all personal responsibility for the borderline between sense and nonsense, 'but if you take a penny and roll it along the top of the desk – like that – the date is more or less on the circumference, like A, and Britannia's topless –'

'That will do, all of you!' I said sharply.

'– some other bit of it, further in, is X, sir. Well, then, when the date has come round to the bottom again – whoops! she nearly went – right round again, sir, the other bit, X, comes with it, so they're both back where they started, only further on, if you see what I mean, sir.'

'Well?'

'Well, they've travelled together, sir, so one of them can't possibly get left behind.'

In my younger days, when a boy delivered himself of some nonsensical taradiddle and then sat waiting for praise with a look of pleased expectancy on his face, I was sometimes hard put to it not to remove that look by any means that lay to hand. With the years one learns, if not acceptance, at least resignation. There is nothing for it but just to soldier on.

'To re-state a problem, Henderson,' I said slowly, raising my head from lightly clenched fists, 'in more clumsy terms than those in which it was originally put is not an explanation of that problem. The whole difficulty –. Put that money away at once, Blake, and tell him what the difficulty is.'

'Me, sir?'

'Yes, you, Blake. Or have you by any chance got left behind on the Inner Circle?'

When the laughter had died down Blake, rather to my surprise, gave a very fair account of our little paradox, simply reiterating that, when a wheel rotates, any point within it describes a smaller circle round the centre than a point on the circumference of the wheel, i.e. it travels a shorter distance. Why then does it not get left behind?

'Oh that,' Henderson said. 'I suppose the inner bit goes faster because it's nearer the middle part that actually turns, the axle, sir.'

'So it gets there first?'

'Er – no, sir. Not exactly. Things sort of even up I expect.'

'You mean that X travels faster over a shorter distance and so keeps pace with A which travels more slowly over a longer distance? Is that how you resolve the difficulty, Henderson?'

Watching the boy nodding his head with every appearance of relief, I was reminded of a conversation I had had with his father at half-term. 'I am very anxious –' Henderson Senior had been good enough to tell me '– my wife and I are most anxious that Dick should not be held back. He is an intelligent boy, you know, Mr Wentworth, and we are sometimes a little afraid that the pace of the majority. . . .' And so on. And so on. The pace of the majority, eh? Mustn't get in the way of the fliers, must we? One realizes the difficulties, of course, but if the boy could be given his head. . . .

'Sir, actually, sir, the outside goes faster than the inside, doesn't it, sir?'

'It does, Potter, it does,' I said. 'The Earth's axis rotates once in twenty-four hours, and Burgrove School travels at a rate of about a thousand miles an hour, so we shall probably agree that we are all going round a great deal faster than a man at the North Pole. What is the matter now, Mason?'

Mason said that he felt giddy, and my first inclination was to tell him not to try to be funny. But I remember, years ago, giving fifty lines to a boy who complained of a headache when we were tackling a problem about hammering nails into a wall, and it turned out afterwards that he was sickening for measles, which led to a tiresome talk with the Headmaster. Schoolmastering is not as cut and dried a business as some people would have us believe. So I told Mason he had better go and see Matron during break.

'I don't see what *she* can do about it,' Potter said.

'She could send him to the North Pole,' some fool suggested.

'That will do, all of you,' I told them, in a voice that made it pretty clear that I was not in a mood for any nonsense. 'And stop snapping your fingers at once, Henderson.'

'Sir, I was only going to say, sir, that if the parts that have furthest to go travel faster than the bits that travel slower – the inside bits, sir – it's no wonder they all get there at the same time. I don't quite see the difficulty.'

A moment or two later the bell rang, rather to my relief, and some of the boys who did see the difficulty crowded round my desk complaining that I had not given them the answer. One of them asked me if we could go on with it next time, and though I am always on my guard against the little monkeys' attempts to trail red herrings in front of me I merely told him that we should have to see. The object of education is to get boys to think for themselves, or so I believe. To start one or two of them wondering about the properties of moving circles is *not* a waste of time, whatever some of my colleagues may think. At any rate, several of my IIIA boys, I noticed, were rolling pennies about during break, until Raikes told them to stop.

'A rolling penny gathers no moss,' I reminded him, but he made a quite inconsequent reply. I fear he is altogether too self-assured, to put it mildly, to take advice from a very much older hand.

A Nature Ramble

I have nothing against Botany, in its proper place. Those who care to interest themselves in stipules and so forth are at liberty to do so. But I know nothing of such things and am not qualified, as I told the Headmaster, to conduct a Botany Ramble – certainly not during school hours, which were never intended to be spent fooling about in woods.

There is a great deal too much of this broader education as they call it, in my opinion. The boys spend half their time visiting art galleries and magistrate's courts, when they aren't gaping at television pictures of irrigation methods in the Sudan. An excursion to the Cheddar Caves cannot be turned into work just by putting 'Geology' in front of it in the School Calendar. This kind of thing was kept for the holidays in my young days, and the only result of spending time on it when the boys ought to be busy with their history books or with ruler and pencil is that I frequently catch them working in their leisure time – which used to be considered unhealthy. I spoke up about it at the last Masters' Meeting, suggesting that a visit to Brewster Sessions would be of educational value to the eleven-year-olds, and the Headmaster said he would make a note of it. Apparently it never crossed his mind that I was speaking ironically.

My clearly expressed wish not to take the Botany class out was brushed aside, 'Raikes has to get the gym ready for Madrigals,' the Headmaster said brusquely. (Madrigals in the gym, eh? For two pins I would have retorted that *I* had to move the parallel bars into the chapel for Muscular Christianity.) 'Anyway, there is nothing in it. The boys make their own plans about what they are going to collect and – and so on. All you have to do is to supervise. So be a good chap'.

Be a good chap indeed! Exactly what that Colonel Ripley used to say, when something unpleasant was in the wind.

As a matter of fact there was such a big turn-out for the Ramble after the news got about that I was to take it – twice the usual number, Gilbert told me – that I could not help a feeling of quiet satisfaction. Popularity is a thing that no schoolmaster worth his salt cares a rap about but I sometimes think that Raikes rather overdoes the hail-fellow attitude. ('When you eventually leave us, Raikes,' I remember Taylor saying one day in break, 'to become a Regional Youth Leader, the phrase "He entered fully into the life of the School" will undoubtedly appear in *The Burgrovian*. One hopes it will be ample reward for all this rushing about in shorts and crying "Come on, chaps!"' Taylor tends to be a little harsh at times, but he puts things so well that one is apt to laugh first and frown afterwards, which is not the way to suppress him.) So it was difficult, as I say, when one saw so many boys milling about with their collecting boxes, especially as Raikes himself happened to come by with a music-stand and what Taylor describes as that 'on the job' look – well anyway, stipules or no stipules, I set out on this absurd Ramble in better humour than I had expected.

We had not got far from the school, taking the field path to Amberley Wood, when a small boy came running back to me with the lower jaw of a sheep clutched in his hand. I make a point of knowing every boy by name, but some of the younger ones occasionally catch me out.

'It's Coutts, isn't it?' I said, after a moment's thought.

'I think it's part of a sheep,' he said. 'Oh, I see what you mean, sir. I'm Betterton, R. B.'

'Well, Betterton, R. B.,' I said with a smile. 'What can I do for you?'

I understood him to say that he thought I should be interested in his specimen, and as he looked genuinely rueful I affected a concern in his unappetizing relic.

'Though it scarcely comes under Botany, does it, Betterton?' I added.

'No, sir. At least – no, sir.'

The boy was clearly bewildered, and when I asked him what particular plants, or aspects of botany he was supposed to be studying that afternoon, admitted that he wasn't 'quite sure'. So I called to Barstow, who was eating grass nearby, and inquired what they were all meant to be doing. Barstow is in my mathematical set and not unintelligent, as boys go, but all he was able to tell me was 'Botany, sir. Sort of general botany. You know, sir' – which is about what I should expect when the boys, in the Headmaster's grandiose phrase, 'make their own plans'. Still, there it was.

'Run along then and do sort of general botany, Betterton,' I said. 'Collect things. Specimens, boy.'

'What sort of specimens, sir?'

'Goodness me,' I said. 'How should I know? Anything that Mr Raikes has taught you about. Lush eglantine. Green cowbind and the moonlight-coloured may. *I* don't know.'

'Lush eglantine, sir?'

'Mr Raikes hasn't told us anything about that, sir.'

'Very likely not, Barstow,' I said. 'But Shelley has. Somebody has told you about Shelley, I suppose? "And in the warm hedge grew lush eglantine, Green cowbind . . .".'

Betterton, who seems to be a boy without initiative, said that he didn't know what eglantine looked like, and Barstow told him it was lush. 'Look for it in warm hedges,' somebody else suggested; and to my surprise I found that quite a little knot had collected round us. 'There grew pied wind-flowers,' I quoted, hardly realizing that I was speaking aloud, 'and – let me see, yes –

> *There grew pied wind-flowers and violets,*
> *Daisies, those pearled Arcturi of the earth*
> *The constellated flower that never sets;*
> *Faint oxlips; tender bluebells, at whose birth*
> . . . *The* something something tumte tumte *wets.*

'Golly!' some young ass said, and put the rest of it out of my mind.

'Off you go, all of you,' I ordered. 'And leave Hopgood's cap alone, Blake. This is in school hours, you know.' School hours indeed! What on earth has all this nonsense to do with Common Entrance and the serious things of life?

I had hoped to be left to my own devices for the rest of the Ramble, but one gets used to disappointments at this game. Pretty soon I heard one boy shout to another, 'Is it true they've got to be Shelley?' and the other called back, 'It's crackers. I don't know any.' Then somebody else – I think it was Huntly, who needs a haircut – joined in with 'What about Keats? The Eager Beaver made us learn a bit beginning

Open afresh your round of starry folds,
Ye ardent marigolds.

Anybody seen any ardent marigolds around these parts?' And in next to no time the whole pack of them were shouting 'Bags I Wordsworth!', 'Any dandelions in *The Ancient Mariner*?', and even more childish rubbish that I do not care to repeat. If boys can possibly get hold of the wrong end of the stick, or start a rumour out of nothing, they will do so. Still, it was no business of mine – or so I thought until young Wrigley came running up to me crying 'Sir! Sir, what was there on the bank besides wild thyme, sir?'

'What is all this nonsense, Wrigley?' I said.

'Well, I thought – they said you said. . . .'

'I said nothing, Wrigley.'

'It isn't fair,' he said, hardly troubling to listen to me. 'Some of them know masses. I had to do *Maud* last term, only Henderson says it's garden flowers and doesn't count. A fat chance anyway,' he said, getting quite shrill, 'of finding larkspurs in this sort of. . . .'

'Be quiet, Wrigley!' I ordered. I had heard quite enough for one thing, and for another some kind of hullabaloo had broken out in a clump of rhododendrons. I strode across to put a stop to it and found a boy called Greaves apparently trying to put a much smaller boy down a rabbit hole.

'Get up at once, both of you,' I cried. 'Greaves, you should be ashamed of yourself.'

'He pinched my pied wind-flower,' Greaves said sulkily.

'Wind-flower my foot,' the small boy said, pulling his jersey clear of his mouth. 'It's glabrous.'

I saw that it was high time to take charge. 'Wipe that fungus off your collar and tell everybody to come here at once,' I told Greaves. 'As for you, Coutts –'

'I'm Betterton, R. B.,' he interrupted.

'Never mind that,' I said. I spoke perhaps more sharply than was altogether justified; but I rarely make the same mistake twice in one day, and the circumstance nettled me. Nor, to be fair to myself, was it necessary for him, as far as I could see, to add his initials every time in that rather pert way.

'Now listen to me, Betterton, R. B.,' I said, ' – though it is news to me that there is another Betterton in the School –'

'I had a brother here, sir,' he put in. 'Betterton, C. A. Before your time, sir.'

'*Before my time*!' I thundered. 'Indeed, Betterton? Before my time, eh? Well, it may interest you to know . . .'

However, the other boys were beginning to gather round us, and I decided to wait for a better opportunity to make young Betterton, R. B. understand that a boy had to be at least as old as his father to be before my time at Burgrove. Older, in fact. Why, when I first came here, the sycamore outside the San was no more than a sapling – a little thing that you could trip over, as I well remember – and eventually it grew so big that it overshadowed the upper windows. 'I'm afraid your brother won't remember the day it had to be cut down,' I shall tell young Betterton. 'It was before his time.' There is no harm in scoring off the young fellows, once in a while.

Some of the boys pretended to be disappointed when I made it clear to them that whoever had started this idea of 'poetic posies', as I called it, it certainly was not I. One or two of them tried to press bindweed and celandine and similar rubbish upon me, and Mason, who is not always very clever at drawing the line between good-humoured fun and downright impertinence, brought up a blade of wheat and asked whether it could be the alien corn that Ruth was sick for home in. I told them all, pretty firmly, to get on with whatever it was they had planned to do before the Ramble started, and to rejoin me in forty minutes, sharp. 'Before it *started*?' Mason asked, but he got no change out of me. 'Now, be off with you,' I said, and when at last they had straggled away, I sat down on an old tree trunk, lit my pipe and settled down for a little peace. It was pleasant in the wood, and I suppose the surroundings influenced my thoughts. At any rate, I felt contented with my job, taking one thing with another. They're a likeable lot,' I caught myself thinking. 'No real harm in them.' Though 'most of them' would be nearer the mark. One has to beware of getting softer as the years go by.

An Hour of English

Gilbert asked me out of the blue this morning to take his lot in English after break, while he went to the dentist.

One is expected to be Jack of all Trades in this business. A banker would make a fine to-do if he were suddenly switched to fishmongering for an hour, and I dare say a nuclear physicist might not relish a short spell on the Bench. Cabinet Ministers, it is true, are sometimes shuffled about from one subject to another and back again almost as rapidly as we are, but they do *not*, I imagine, have to take charge from the word Go in their new department. Civil servants can presumably be left to get on with their work without supervision, while the new man settles in – which is emphatically not the case with boys. However, one is used to it by this time and all I said was 'Oh. Well. It's not very – oh, very well then. Where have they got to?'

'*Got* to?' he repeated. 'English isn't quite like Algebra, you know. We don't finish Exercise 25 and then turn over to Exercise 26, if that's what you mean.'

'No,' I said warmly. 'I do not doubt that it is all very vague and woolly. Still, there must be some sort of system, I suppose? There must be a few things that your boys have learned, and a very great many that they have not. Or may I take it that the field is absolutely clear, that I can safely start from the very beginning?'

'What *is* the very beginning of English, would you say?' put in young Raikes, with his insufferable air of scoring over a much older man.

'Parsing and the construction of sentences,' I rapped out without a moment's hesitation, and took my gown off its hook to show that I had more important things to do than waste time on a very indifferent Third (so I hear) in Part II of the Geography Tripos.

'Good God!' he said, resorting to rudeness and blasphemy, as the modern generation so often do when properly floored in an argument.

'Look, A.J.,' Gilbert said. 'If you are going to be kind enough to take the little devils, just read them a bit of poetry or prose and then discuss it with them. Or get them to read it, if you like. It takes longer.'

'Can you be sure of that?' Raikes said.

'As you wish, Gilbert,' I said, deliberately taking no notice of the interruption, and I went off in no very good temper to wrestle – or rather, since the word gives a wrong impression, to knock the elements of trionomial factorization into the heads of my own IIIA. It is all very well to sneer about Exercise 26 (and we have got to No. 42, as it happens), but we do at least know where we are going next. We may move slowly in IIIA, but we *progress*. Gilbert and his lot, so far as I can make out, do not even know where they have *been*.

'Good morning,' I said, strolling casually after break into Lower IV's classroom and silencing the excited buzz that greeted my unexpected arrival. 'Mr Gilbert has gone to the dentist's. So we are to have the pleasure of each other's company for an hour. What is the case of "the dentist's" in that sentence – er, Coutts?'

'I'm Betterton, R. B., sir,' said the boy my eye had fallen on. 'Brother of –'

'Brother of Betterton, C. A.' I put in quickly. 'Who was here before I was born, eh? Exactly. Well, Betterton, R. B., as Coutts is not with us –'

'Sir, but I am, sir. I'm here, sir,' shouted a ginger-haired boy, whose name I could have sworn was Cunningham. In the old days I very soon had them all sorted out; but of course the School numbers have gone up from about seventy to over a hundred, which would account for it.

'That will do, Coutts, thank you,' I said quietly. 'There is no need to make a noise. Now, Betterton, perhaps you can forget your aged brother for a moment and tell me what "the dentist's" case is.'

'The dentist's case, sir?' Betterton repeated, staring at me with his mouth open as if I had taken leave of my senses. 'Well, I suppose it's Mr Gilbert, sir, at present. Is that what you meant, sir?'

I made no very serious attempt to check the burst of laughter, believing that it does a boy no harm to be made to realize, now and again, that he has made a fool of himself. And by the time it subsided I had made up my mind that it would be a waste of time, if Betterton was a fair specimen of the Form's intelligence, to take up grammatical points with them. Before one can usefully come to grips with an unfamiliar lot of boys it is essential to find out what they know – not a very lengthy process in my experience – so I began with a few very general questions to test them.

'Give me the name of any three English dramatists, not counting Shakespeare,' I said.

'Not counting Shakespeare, sir?'

'That is what I said, Lovejoy. Come along, come along, all of you. Wake up!'

They stared at me like so many sheep.

'Playwrights,' I said. 'People who wrote plays. Surely some of you have heard of Sheridan and Marlowe? Just give me their names – and stop playing with that penknife, Coutts.'

'Not counting Sheridan and Marlowe, sir?'

'Naturally,' I said.

'That's three already we can't count, counting Shakespeare,' Betterton objected. 'It certainly makes it pretty difficult.'

'It means we'll have to know six altogether,' Lovejoy agreed, 'by the time we've got three more. That's twice as many –'

'Sophocles!' shouted a small freckled boy at the back.

I settled his hash with a look and began to tap significantly on my desk with the blunt end of a pencil. 'My goodness me,' I cried. 'Out of all the world-famous –'

'Agatha Christie,' some fool volunteered.

'Twelfth Fabulous Year,' another boy added. 'You can't say she doesn't count.'

'Shattering, actually,' put in Thwaites. 'Fabulous is *Oliver*.'

'That will do,' I rapped out, not being able to make head nor tail of what they were talking about. 'As dramatists hardly seem to be your strong point, we had better try novelists. Has anybody here heard of Dickens?'

Several boys put up their hands, but one of them had the impertinence to accuse me of unfairness. 'I was just going to say "Dickens",' he said, 'and now you've gone and spoilt it.'

'Stand up at once,' I told him. 'Blake, isn't it? Exactly. Aren't you the boy I had to speak to the other day for fooling about with Hopgood's cap? Well, let me make one thing clear to you, young Blake –'

'Ask to have thirteen other offences taken into consideration,' somebody whispered, but I wasn't quite quick enough to nail down the culprit.

'Get this into your thick head, young Blake – and all the rest of you. If you think I am the kind of man to put up with any nonsense you are making a thundering big mistake. If there is one more inter – Coutts!'

'Sir?'

'Did I not tell you to stop playing about with that penknife?'

'This is a nail file, sir,' he explained, showing it to me.

'Put it away,' I ordered. 'You have all a very great deal to learn, and the sooner you realize it and get down to some good hard work the better. You seem to have little or no knowledge of our great dramatists and novelists, and as for poets, I do not doubt –'

'Blake!' shouted Betterton, so loudly that the boy of that name nearly jumped out of his skin and said 'I'm sorry, sir. I was only –'

There was a general laugh at this, in which, after a moment's hesitation, I joined. 'I think Betterton was referring to Blake, W.,' I said mildly. 'Rather before your time, Blake, C. D. – and even before your brother's, eh, Betterton?'

Betterton had the grace to look a little silly over this reference to the brush we had on the Botany Ramble, and pretty soon afterwards he and all the others settled down to listen quietly while I read them a few suitable extracts from the *Odyssey*. In translation, of course.

'Who *was* Homer, sir?' one little chap asked me eagerly, just as the bell went, unfortunately.

'Aha.' I said. 'Now that *is* a question. Some say that he was a blind poet from the island of Chios; others that he was really many men rolled into one.'

'Golly!' said Coutts, who was listening, like most of the others. 'So if you asked us for the names of half-a-dozen Greek poets, Homer might do for the lot?'

'Oh run along with you,' I said. But I could not help grinning all the same. Teaching can be quite fun, sometimes.

Not a Fulbright Exactly

I have had some surprises in my life, not counting the time I was accused of attacking a boy with a cutlass during the after-lunch rest period, but I have rarely been more astonished than when the Headmaster stopped me on my way down the school corridor to take IIIA in Algebra and asked me whether I would like to go to America. I was already a couple of minutes late owing to a trivial mishap in the Common Room and not really in the mood for aimless conversation.

'Generous as is the scale of pay for assistant masters,' I began, trying to keep any trace of irony out of my voice, 'it still does not permit –'

'Your gown is on inside out,' he said.

'That may well be, Headmaster,' I replied with some warmth. 'If a little more time were allowed us between Chapel and Morning School and if, furthermore, adequate illumination could be provided in the cupboard in the Common Room, I dare say one might contrive to be properly dressed in time for – for gossiping in the corridors during working hours, let us say.'

'No, seriously, Wentworth,' he said, helping me off with the gown, which turned out, as I might have guessed, to be Rawlinson's. 'If you would like a week or two in the States, it's in the bag.'

'Bag?' I repeated, still half suspecting a leg-pull. The Reverend Gregory Saunders, though a sound administrator and an Oxford M.A. to boot, has a sense of humour that sometimes gets the better of him (not perhaps, as my colleague Gilbert once remarked, a really Herculean task), so that one has learned over the years to be a little wary.

However, he soon convinced me that he was indeed serious on this occasion. Some sort of Fund existed, he explained, with the object of arranging exchange visits between British and American teachers, and my name had been put forward for one of these so-called Fellowships – not a Fulbright or a Guggenheim exactly –

'No, no,' I put in.

– in view of my long experience of English preparatory schools and also, no doubt, because the publication in America of some jottings of mine about life at Burgrove had created something of a stir in educational circles over there. 'They know what to expect, you see,' the Headmaster ended, with a smile.

'Oh come!' I said. 'That was years ago.'

'Well, there it is,' he said. 'All found, and practically nothing to do. The details are in this pamphlet. Think it over.'

I thanked him and said I should certainly do so, though my mind was already made up. When something comes along that seems too good to be true one naturally says yes, even though it may turn out not to be. I am to do no teaching apparently, it is not that kind of exchange; merely give one or two talks here and there. Otherwise my time is my own, to go where I like, the idea being, of course, to gain knowledge of each other's countries, spread mutual understanding and so forth, which I dare say I can do as well as the next man, or better in a good many cases. It is absurd to be so excited at my age, but upon my soul I could hardly do justice to the school lunch (which reminds me of another good thing of Gilbert's, about the beef one Summer term in the old days. What was it? 'Do justice to it?' he said – not in the boys' hearing, naturally. 'I'd give it ten years hard, if it hadn't so obviously had that already.' Still, that is by the way). I shall have to pull myself together and get down to some serious planning. One has to be vaccinated, I see from the pamphlet, which I suppose means that there is a lot of smallpox over there. Clothing is a worry in view of the extremes of climate to be expected in so large a continent.

One does not want to be snowbound in an alpaca jacket, particularly when one is travelling as one's country's representative, up to a point. There is a visa to be got, and I suppose I ought to take a cap for the sea voyage. One way and another there is a great deal to do.

The news has already spread, as I feared it would, and it is difficult to get any good work out of the boys. There was a perfect chorus of questions as soon as I set foot in IIIA this morning:

'Sir, is it true, sir?'

'Sir, are you going in a 707?'

'Is it true they're all very grown-up in their schools and don't learn anything, sir?'

'It's funny, my father says nobody speaks to anybody if they've got more money, practically, than the other person, isn't it, sir?'

'Will you be going to Arkansas, sir, because I know someone whose sister –'

'It's Arkansaw, Squiffy – with the accent on the Ark.'

'As in Noah's time?'

'Steady!' I said, raising a hand for silence. 'One at a time, now. One at a time. Though you seem to know all about it already; some of you. Yes, Mason? Did you say something?'

'No, sir,' he said. 'Except the only thing is if you get knocked down in a fight you want to lie on your back and with your knees doubled up and then when he jumps on you kind of hollow your back and hoosh out with your legs so that he reels right back across the saloon and ends up against the far wall with about a million bottles on his head.'

'I see,' I said, when the laughter had subsided. 'Thank you, Mason. But I think my saloon-fighting days are over. And now, if nobody else has any advice to offer, perhaps we might turn our attention to the Remainder Theorem.'

As a matter of fact, quite a number of them genuinely wanted to know more about America, and I had to rap sharply on my desk in order to keep the discussion within bounds. Many masters of my acquaintance would not have permitted a digression of this kind, but in my experience when boys are a bit excited it is wise to allow them to let off steam. They work all the better for it afterwards, if any time is left. A further point is, as I often try to explain to Rawlinson when he complains of the noise disturbing his History classes, that eagerness to learn is always to be encouraged, and there are more things in the world than algebra and geometry. I have always been a firm believer in the value of a broad general education, a term which must surely include some knowledge of the great and friendly Republic across the Atlantic. Many of the questions put to me this morning, which I shall be in a position to answer more fully when I return from my visit, showed a woeful ignorance of American life and manners. All in all, I rose from my desk when the bell rang with a greatly strengthened conviction of the benefits my forthcoming trip would bring not only to myself but to the School. It was a considerable satisfaction to be able to turn aside young Wrigley's final question with a quiet 'I'll tell you all about that when I come back.' No schoolmaster cares to admit that he is uncertain whether Cole Slaw is the name of a songwriter or of a headland up in New England.

'They are extremely frank and outspoken about their own shortcomings, but by the same token they do not relish criticism from outsiders. Remember that, Wentworth!'

If the Headmaster has a fault it is a tendency to teach his grandmother to suck eggs. I suppose I am the last man in the world to barge about a foreign country pointing out their errors, however sore the temptation. The English are far too inclined to feel superior to other races, and I am determined during my stay in the United States to behave as I should at home, dress quietly, observe, listen courteously, and speak little and with reserve. The contrast will be there for them, if they have eyes to see. As to their frankness about their own national faults, which I ha certainly often noted in books and films, if the same th comes out in conversation I suppose the wisest cour be to look dubious, without openly or rudely contra

One can hardly, in a short visit, affect to know more about their habits than they do themselves. At any rate I shall know how to conduct myself, I fancy, without any assistance from the Headmaster.

'I have already had the benefit of some advice from Mason,' I told him irritably, 'and of the two –'

'Advice from *Mason*!' he exclaimed. 'What was that, Wentworth?'

'It is of no consequence,' I said, rather regretting that I had been led to mention the matter.

'Advice from Mason, eh?' he repeated. 'About what exactly?'

'The boy gets over-excited at times,' I said. 'But he has made better progress this term, and I have hopes –'

'No, no, Wentworth,' he said. 'I insist upon knowing.'

'It was nothing. Nothing at all. Some nonsense about lying on my back in saloons with my knees doubled up and – ah – hooshing – I really forget. If I had known you would be so interested, Headmaster. . . .'

'Hooshing?' he repeated, with that annoying habit of picking up a single word out of a sentence. 'And do you intend to follow this advice, Wentworth?'

'I think, if you don't mind, I ought to be getting on with my arrangements,' I said turning away. 'There is a great deal to do.'

'Hooshing *what*?' he called after me.

'Hooshing my legs, of course,' I shouted, in a sudden fury, and strode through the swing door, almost colliding with Matron who gave me an inquisitive look. It is petty annoyances of this kind, which seem to be inseparable from school life at Burgrove, that make me look forward so keenly to wider horizons across the seas. But for the itching of my vaccination scar it would be difficult to realize that in a little over a week from now the Statue of Liberty and I will be abreast.

Interlude in America

Preparing for the West

I always think it best to prepare myself, so far as may be, for any new experience. Some people argue that the slate should be wiped clean, so that it is ready for new impressions instead of being cluttered up with preconceptions and so on. But I don't know. I have seen a good many clean slates in my time as a schoolmaster, and most of them were not notably quick at receiving impressions. I suppose I mean wax rather than slate, but the sense is clear enough. One can have an open mind without its being entirely empty, and I never dream of going to Switzerland or Scotland or anywhere a bit out of the way without looking up the heights of the mountains in advance and reading about William Tell and Bonnie Prince Charlie. The natives can pull your leg unmercifully, for one thing, unless you have a few facts to check them by. For another, people are not always as well-informed about their own country as you might expect. I remember, years ago, telling a French acquaintance at Poitiers that Edward the Black Prince routed sixty thousand Frenchmen near there in 1356, although outnumbered by five to one – a thing he might not have known to this day, if I had not taken the trouble to look it up beforehand. I certainly don't intend to travel up and down America in a state of open-mouthed astonishment at everything I see and hear.

Friends have been most helpful in suggesting useful books to give me a foretaste of the general tone, the *ethos*, of the place. I have dipped into novels by William Faulkner and Marquand, looked more briefly at the work of a man called Cozens who, one must hope, does not give a representative picture, and of course refreshed my memory of

Huckleberry Finn. I have also read widely in a book called *Inside U.S.A.*, kindly lent me by the Headmaster, which confirmed my belief that there is much in American life that would scarcely do over here. The author, a Mr John Gunther, constantly asks 'Who runs Nebraska?' and suchlike questions, leaving me a little bewildered. What on earth would one say if one were asked who runs Birmingham? Or Yorkshire? Still, there is a mass of information which no doubt will come in handy as I travel about. I shall take it with me, I think, for reference – unless I find that the *World Almanack* for 1955, which I confiscated this morning from Wrigley, will do instead. What on earth the boy was doing with such a thing in his possession I am at a loss to understand. It has a distinct American bias, being published I see in New York, and gives, to take an example at random, the number of Hungarian-born whites in North Dakota in 1950, which you would never find in a truly 'world' almanack published, say, in London. In the ordinary way, when boys are caught playing with darts, transistor sets and so on during working hours, we masters return the confiscated article after a few hours or days, according to the seriousness of the offence, but I do not feel that Wrigley will have any right to complain if I retain this almanack a little longer. Does the boy think that Burgrove is going to enter for one of these deplorable school quizzes on television?

Gilbert wandered into my room while I was conning over my collection of books and agreed that they ought to make a pretty good general introduction to the American scene. 'For instance,' he said, flipping one or two of them open at random, 'if you happen to find yourself floating down the Mississippi on a raft, with a man like Willis Wayde aboard, it will be useful to know that Stewart Thompson, of Yale, threw the discus 162 feet 7½ inches at the 20th Annual Heptagonal Track and Field Championships, Cambridge, Mass., on May 15th, 1954.'

'Yes, yes,' I said. 'Put that Almanack down, there's a good chap. It isn't mine.'

'"Oshkosh is known for overalls, trucks, motors and luggage,"' he read. 'You'll knock the Yanks for six all right, when you pass that bit of information on. "Wisconsin has 10,000 miles of trout streams, 8,500 lakes with sturgeon, muskellunge, pike, bass, perch, smelts. Hunting – as you know, Mrs Mulheimer – includes deer, bear, red fox, raccoon. . . ." They're going to go crazy over your light conversation, A.J.'

'I have a lot to do, if you will forgive me, Gilbert,' I said, not being in the mood for this kind of foolery. Naturally I am not proposing to cram my mind with a mass of trivial detail, some of which may well be out of date, still less try to pass it on to our good friends on the other side. 'Yanks' indeed! That is just the kind of contemptuous attitude that I am determined not to adopt.

What is 'Sorghum', one wonders? I see that 6,170,000 tons of it were produced for forage as recently as 1953, and another 5,906,000 for silage. Which reminds me that I must be careful to get my billions right over there. One does not want to be too easily impressed through forgetting to knock off the last three noughts.

I suppose, at my age, I ought to be able to take a trip to America in my stride, and so in a way I can. But I confess to a feeling of excitement and exhilaration such as has scarcely visited me since I was chosen to play for my School Hockey XI – and that was a great many years ago. Shall I see Niagara Falls? and the Grand Canyon? I know very little as yet about the actual programme. Apparently I am to meet a Mr Herbert S. Bulkin – 'make contact' is the phrase used, as though we were a couple of electric wires – on my arrival in New York, and he will tell me of the arrangements. So far as there are to be arrangements, that is. I am to be free to make my own plans for at least part of the time, mix with the people and so on. It is not as if I were going to Moscow, with a so-called 'escort' dogging my footsteps to make sure that I took no photographs in the poorer quarters. There are one or two places where I am expected to give talks, and of course I shall want to see something of the educational system over there. But apart from that I shall be a bit of a gipsy, I dare say. The open road, eh? One might even find oneself in Oshkosh one of these fine days. Who knows? It has an un-English ring, overalls or no overalls.

It is difficult, one way and another, to give as much attention as I should like to the humdrum work of the School.

At Sea

There are nineteen coat-hangers in my cabin. One realizes, of course, that life at sea is a very different kettle of fish from life on land, and on the second day out one has hardly had time to sit down and get one's sea-boots on as the saying goes. But even so! I doubt whether there were as many as nineteen in the whole of Burgrove, excluding the Matron's which I have naturally not counted. I have also got ten light-switches, apart altogether from the bathroom, which is full of towels – two bath towels and from four to eight face towels. It is difficult to be more precise, because whenever I damp one, or even disarrange it, the steward takes it away and brings two more. One dislikes causing trouble, but even when I pat my hands lightly against the inside of the towel without unfolding it, he notices, and takes it away. Rich people are used to this sort of thing, I dare say, but I would just as soon hold my hands out of the port-hole and let them dry in the breeze as make all this fuss and pother every time I wash. Actually, one is warned not to open the scuttle oneself but to send for the steward, so it would be cutting off his nose to spite his face really.

The steward came in as I was jotting down these first impressions of life at sea, so I showed him the coat-hangers and asked him what the idea was. He said the idea was to hang coats on them – not meaning to be impertinent, I think, for he is a civil and well-spoken fellow, but misunderstanding my drift.

'Exactly,' I said. 'But why nineteen?'

To my embarrassment he suspected a complaint and would have brought another half-dozen had I not stopped him in time. Apparently people do make complaints from time to time on these ships, ludicrous as the idea may seem to anyone accustomed to life on the pay of an assistant master.

'Surely,' I asked, to make my point clearer, 'people don't cross the Atlantic with nineteen coats? Not in this direction, anyway.'

He said I should be surprised what some people crossed the Atlantic with, and not quite knowing what he meant I left him and went up to the sun-deck, where I was handed a cup of broth. There seems no end to the luxury and thoughtfulness on these great ships.

After the broth, I went and looked at the Atlantic. It is surprisingly black near the ship when you look down, except where it is churned up and frothing and so on; but further off it is green – unless the sun is shining, in which case it is blue as at Broadstairs. I mention this because people who have never crossed the Atlantic may think they are missing something, whereas in fact it is much the same in the middle as it is at the edges, though deeper naturally. Still, one looks at it a good deal.

One of the funnels is full of old rope. I discovered this quite by chance while up on the top deck wondering whether Mrs Duval expected an apology.* A sailor opened a door in the side of one of these huge flues and disappeared from sight under my very eyes. Naturally I thought he had fallen down into whatever it is the funnel is connected to below, and was on the point of raising a cry of 'Man down the funnel!' or whatever was appropriate when he reappeared with a length of cable and a broom. I could hardly have been more astonished if I had seen the vicar back at home take a bottle of port out of one of the organ pipes.

I mentioned the incident to the purser, who took it very lightly. It was quite a normal thing, he said, to have a false funnel, and he explained that when this ship was built passengers thought a single funnel was a bit *infra dig*. 'Besides,' he said, 'she looks better with two.'

* I have asked Mr Wentworth to explain this allusion, but he declines.

I must say I thought it sailing a bit close to the wind.

'Supposing they started doing the same sort of thing with railway engines?' I said. 'Or motor cars and so on?'

He said that cars no longer had funnels, a fact of which I did not need to be reminded. 'I am speaking generally,' I said. 'If I were to buy a six-cylinder car, I certainly should not expect to find that two of the cylinders were intended for the storage of bits of rag, spare nuts and bolts and so on. Is not the parallel disturbingly close?'

The purser said he thought not. No deception was intended. The ship was not at present in the market, but if at any time she was put up for sale he felt sure the Company would include 'one dummy funnel' in the specification. Meanwhile 'it isn't as if we blew dummy smoke through it,' he added, with what seemed to me an odd confusion of thought.

I don't know what to think, I am sure. It would be a fine thing if half the lifeboats turned out to be made of cardboard and only put there because they made the passengers feel safer. I put this point to a man at my table called Rumbolt, who is quite an experienced traveller, and he said it was all over the ship that I was claiming a reduction for misrepresentation of funnels. 'You ought to come back on one of the *Queens*,' he said. 'They carry two captains.' I could make no sense of this remark. Surely he doesn't mean that one of *them* is a dummy?

I am tired of being told to 'wait until you see the New York skyline'. One has no option. If it was Americans who made the remark I could understand and sympathize; one naturally likes to make the best of one's own country in advance. But the worst offender is Rumbolt, who is as English as I am. He is simply being the patronizing 'old hand', and will no doubt take all the credit for the view when we *do* see it. Just because he has seen these skyscrapers before he seems to be under the impression that he put them up himself – just as old Rawlinson used to say 'Why don't you go to my dear Provence next hols?' on the strength of ten days there, seven of which I know for a fact he spent in a hospital at Orange.

Somebody sighted a whale yesterday, but I was asleep.

Thick fog from the Nantucket Lightship onwards. So the New York skyline was neither more nor less impressive than a row of beans at midnight. I should have been sorry about this, but for Rumbolt. 'Never known such a thing in all my fifty-four crossings,' he said. 'You don't know what you're missing.'

'Is this your *fifty-fourth* crossing?' I asked in amazement.

'It is and all, boy,' he said.

'In that case,' I replied, with as much calmness as I could muster after being addressed in such a fashion, 'surely you must have started from the wrong side?'

'When I say "crossing",' he explained airily, 'I mean of course the double event – there and back, boy, there and back.'

Well! I am the last person to make a hasty or unkind judgement, but I am bound to say that had he been a member of my IIIA Mathematics set I should have told him that the only honourable thing to do when caught out in a lie is to own up. I hardly think he is the kind of person to be a successful 'unofficial ambassador' (which, in a sense, one is here) in a country where tact and a determination to treat people as equals are of such vital importance.

Perhaps fortunately, I was saved from the necessity of replying by the intervention of an American who pointed out to me the Statue of Liberty, just discernible through the murk.

'Why, it's tiny!' I cried involuntarily, adding, in case he should think I was in any way belittling the famous symbol, 'Not that mere size is of any significance. We Englishmen have at least, in a thousand years of history, learnt *that*.'

'I certainly trust,' he said after a pause, 'that you will have a fruitful and interesting stay in my large young country, Mr Wentworth.' There is a grave courtesy about the best type of American that is altogether refreshing and delightful.

I cannot say the same for the Customs man, whose manner I thought decidedly offhand. I told him very politely that I had nothing of value in my luggage – unless, I added with a smile, some notes for a talk on education in England could be so described. He simply pointed to one of my bags and said 'That one!'

'I am British,' I said, speaking slowly and distinctly in case my unfamiliar accent had confused him. 'I have come here by invitation on an exchange basis arranged by – not a Fulbright exactly –'

'Open it up,' he said.

Well, really! Still, there was no help for it, and I was naturally put out when the fellow rummaged about among my shirts and so on, without a with-your-leave or by-your-leave, finally coming up with the bottle of fruit salts without which I never travel. 'What's this then?' he demanded.

I explained as best I could, without going into details which were none of his business, but even then he had to unscrew the top and taste the stuff on the tip of his finger. 'Fizzy', was all he said.

'It takes all salts to make a world,' I told him, thinking a bit of a joke would lighten things up a little. I might as well have been talking about the unitary method to my IIIA boys for all the interest he showed. So I said no more, even when he began to ram my personal possessions back into the case in the reverse order to that in which I had carefully packed them. One does *not* want one's pyjamas right at the bottom.

'Staying long?' he asked me eventually, with an attempt at friendliness, if such it was, that came a great deal too late to mollify me.

'It begins to look like it,' I said. I had him there, I think.

It was a disappointing start, though, after the fog and so on. As a matter of fact, the very first words addressed to me as I stepped off the gangway on to American soil were 'Put that pipe out, you!' Land of the free, eh?

Contacts

Herbert S. Bulkin is unfortunately away in Seattle, Washington – not of course the well-known Washington but the state which was originally named Columbia and was then changed to Washington because of the existence of the District of Columbia in which the other Washington lies. I suspect some muddle-headedness here, though I naturally have better manners than to say so until I get home. Washington, née Columbia, has thirteen community forests, according to the notes I made at Burgrove, which gives an idea of the scale one is up against here, despite the odd wording. At any rate, that is where Mr Bulkin has gone, leaving me high and dry for the moment but for a note which was very thoughtfully waiting for me at my hotel. This put me in touch with a Fergus Henson Junior, who turned out to be in hospital, but someone at his apartment, as they say, whose name I did not quite catch, was most helpful, and as a result of all this I had an interesting talk with a Mr Schnaffler, whom I met at a dinner party given by a Mrs Teeling. I do not know who Mrs Teeling is exactly, but I was taken there by somebody called Ted, who it turned out did not know Mrs Teeling either. This might have been rather awkward, but Ted said that George A. Mopus had fixed it up through a mutual friend and would introduce us all when we got there.

There was nobody at the party called Mopus actually, but Mrs Teeling was most gracious and invited me to spend a week with a Mr and Mrs Riggery of Colorado Springs any time I was over Denver way. American hospitality is quite overwhelming. One cannot help wondering what friends in England would think if Mr and Mrs George Mopus, to take a name at random, turned up for a weekend with them at my suggestion. Still, I suppose if everybody does it it comes to the same thing in the end.

This Mr Schnaffler took me aside when he heard that this was my first visit to the States and warned me very earnestly to remember that all his countrymen still had a great feeling of inferiority when talking to an Englishman. 'It's the background,' he explained. 'We haven't the built-in culture.' He said he really admired the way we English sprinkled our conversation with literary allusions and references and *bon mots*, just casually and not bothering, and went right along talking as though nothing had happened; whereas your American had to do his damnedest to drag up something suitable out of Donne or Congreve or Sterne to keep his end up. He quoted from Cowper and Crabbe and Gibbon and James Joyce to prove his point, and was halfway through a laughing admission about an acquaintance of his who thought the poet Rochester had a mad wife when Mrs Teeling came up to us and said that her other guests were dying to talk with the guest of honour.

'Guest of honour, Mrs Teeling?' I cried. 'I! I'm afraid I am only an unheard-of schoolmaster,' and I explained that in fact I was really looking for a Herbert S. Bulkin, who was in Seattle.

'Remember what I've told you,' Mr Schnaffler called out as I was led away, 'and you'll understand why we Americans are often a bit tongue-tied and awkward when you come over and see us.'

Somebody took my glass out of my hand as I was passing and substituted a full one, and on turning round to protest I found myself face to face with a tall lady in black who took hold of my tie and said 'British. You can't mistake it,' in a surprisingly deep voice. Meanwhile my hostess was saying to someone behind me, 'I want to have you meet Mr Wentworth, an unheard-of schoolmaster from England who has come over to look for a Herbert S. Bulkin in Seattle,' thus putting me in rather a predicament. I turned my head as far as it would go, in an effort to be polite, and became conscious of a man holding a bowl of white matter flecked with green at my elbow. 'Dip,' he commanded me. 'It has a nuance.'

'I cannot dip,' I said on the spur of the moment, gesturing with my two hands, both of which had now by some means became laden with glasses, 'and to beg I am ashamed.'

'They missed that one,' said the voice of Mr Schnaffler out of the press on my left. 'What did I tell you?'

'Upon my soul,' I burst out, scarcely knowing whether I was on my head or my heels, 'You really are a most extraordinary and likeable people!'

Everybody laughed, and presently I found myself sitting on the floor with quite a pretty young girl who said gravely, 'I heard you are looking for a Herbert S. Bulkin, Mr Wentworth?'

'Do you know him?' I asked.

'Never heard of the man,' she told me. 'I think you are wasting your time. There are better things to see in America than Herbert S. Bulkin, *whoever* he is.'

A mood almost of irresponsibility came over me and I told her that in the State of Washington, where Herbert Bulkin had gone, there were thirteen community forests and I hardly cared whether he got lost in all of them. 'It isn't as if I knew the man,' I said, 'except by name; and even that doesn't seem very likely to me.'

'Mr Wentworth's stopped looking for Herbert S. Bulkin,' the girl called out, and there was a general cheer. All in fun, of course. But it is a far cry from Burgrove School, eh?

There was food, I think, and later on Mr Schnaffler very kindly gave me the historical reasons for America's cultural backwardness, citing (if I remember rightly) George Fox's *Journal*, a number of Acts of Parliament, *The Federalist*, William James and the pragmatists, the Munroe Doctrine, Henry Cabot Lodge and Ernest Hemingway. 'But all this is familiar ground to you, Mr Wentworth,' he ended (we were in the kitchen at the time, I recall, pounding up ice). 'What I really wanted to ask you was what is the precise rating just now, over in your country, of James Gould Cozens and Wallace Stevens?'

'Well of course,' I said, with my mind in a whirl, 'it rather depends.'

A Mr Hackbut came up at this point with a cry of 'Aha! "The thrilling regions of thick-ribbéd ice",' but I capped his quotation by remarking 'What we need is a sledded poleaxe on this, eh?'

'There you are, you see!' Mr Schnaffler said.

We all had some more Bourbon, and I remembered a thing of Dr Johnson's which I forget. Altogether a most enjoyable evening. I have a note to ring up a Mrs Theodore Kramm of Los Angeles, though I am not sure what about. However, she will probably know.

Mr Bulkin called – one doesn't say 'rang' here, for some reason – and seemed sorry to hear about Fergus Henson Jr. He has to go on to Denver, being all snarled up just now, to use his own words, with one wild Professor of Comparative Philology who could *not* be less well adjusted. However, he thought he had a couple of talks lined up for me, and was I making out all right meantime?

I asked him, in case he ran across a man called Ginger Brown while he was in Denver, if he could possibly find out whether Mr Brown was really expecting me on Wednesday week, and he said he would make a note of it. 'It is a little confusing,' I explained, 'because Mr and Mrs Riggery of Colorado Springs –'. But he cut me short with a promise to be back inside two days, and then we would soon have everything sorted out.

I suppose I must accommodate myself to the pace of life in this country, but it is a little worrying not to be doing anything definite yet in return for all the money. Still, as Mr Bulkin pointed out before he rang off (called off can hardly be right, surely?), I am moving about and getting to know the natives, which is half the battle.

I had hardly put the receiver down before George Mopus

came through, and as a result I had my first taste of clam juice, which is about the same as sea water drunk through the nose. It is all experience, though. But before that he took me into an Automat, to explain how it worked, and did not seem to believe me when I said we had the same sort of thing in England. 'Now this man is having beans on toast,' he told me, pausing by a table, and I must say I felt a good deal of embarrassment. It is a different matter when the boys are eating at school and the Headmaster says, as he sometimes does when showing parents round, 'They are having roast lamb today, as you see.' People in restaurants are a different kettle of fish. Nobody seemed to mind, though, and the man just went on eating his beans – which is more than the boys can be persuaded to do in similar circumstances. They are all more free and easy over here. People seem to have nothing to hide, and I dare say it is all part of the same thing as having no fences round their gardens and being so ready to talk about their egos.

They are not ashamed of money, either. I am not sure where Mr Mopus fits into the organization that brought me over, if at all. He merely said 'Oh, *that* one!' when I mentioned Herbert S. Bulkin and let the subject drop. But he insisted on paying for our luncheon, and though I naturally averted my eyes when the time came I could not help seeing how he did it. In England it is always an embarrassment – though not one to which a schoolmaster is often subjected – to be paid for at a restaurant table. Americans, instead of fingering one or two flat notes out of a slim wallet in a furtive sort of way, seem to be able to produce rolls of dollars from any part of their person. They strip off half-a-dozen quite openly, leaving plenty; and of course there is the comfort of not being able to tell whether the notes are ones, fives or tens. In England a five-pound note on a plate is unmistakable; and the only people who have rolls in their pockets are bookmakers, coal miners on holiday and, I dare say, car salesmen, with whom I have never lunched. At any rate, I felt quite at my ease while George Mopus was paying, and did not hesitate afterwards to show him, at his request, the little memo I made at the time on an old envelope.

'"Arthur James Wentworth, Esquire, B.A."' he read out. 'Why, surely –'

'It's on the back,' I said. 'It only says "Makes no bones about it".'

'About what?'

'About paying.'

'I see,' he said. But I am not sure that he understood.

'I make little notes about the things that interest me,' I explained. 'Otherwise one forgets.'

'Oh sure, sure,' he said, and we went on to talk of other things. He criticized the late President Roosevelt in a way that seemed to me to show a lack of proper respect. It is my firm resolve not to interfere in any way in the internal politics of a country where I am a guest, and paid for into the bargain; so I merely remarked, 'In Britain we happen to think he was the greatest President your country has ever had,' and after a glance at my watch to suggest I had another appointment, walked out into the stir and bustle of Fifth Avenue.

Some Impressions of New York

One has read about New York and seen photographs and so on, so that the height of the buildings is not really a surprise, high as they are. One simply looks up, and there they are, and the only surprise in a way is why they stop when they do. It is not as if all of them tapered to a point like the spire of Salisbury Cathedral, which obviously cannot go any further. Still, I am no architect, and no doubt there are reasons – though an Englishman is hard put to it at times to understand why some of the things Americans do are done as they are, unless it is just to be different, which hardly seems worthy of a great democracy. The proper place for a telephone, I should have thought, is a telephone kiosk, not at the back of a shop where it hardly seems fair to make a call without buying something, which I cannot of course afford. This would be a nuisance if one had any calls to make.

I am the last person, I think I may claim, to be accused of insularity or narrow-mindedness, but what is the point of selling you a ticket and then taking it away and giving you another? I was astonished, when making a short train journey from Grand Central station (where the trains are all, rather inconveniently, in the basement – another needless eccentricity), to have my ticket taken from me almost at once by a tall, thin official, who gave me a longer one in exchange; or rather, instead of giving me the longer one he slipped it into a kind of bracket on the back of the seat in front. I said nothing of course, being in a foreign country, and a little later on the same official came back and took the long ticket away, giving me nothing in return. This left me with no ticket at all, whereas the inspector had two, a situation that could never have arisen in my own country. I should certainly not have objected to my original ticket being taken away, for that used to be done on the Great Western many years ago when I was a lad. But to exchange the ticket for another one and then take *that* away is arrant tomfoolery, look at it how you will. It is no part of my business over here to teach the Americans how to run their affairs; otherwise I might well suggest that these ticket exchangers would be better employed as conductors on the New York buses, on which all the work is at present done by the drivers. And what work! Money is put by passengers as they enter into a machine at the driver's right side, which would be sensible enough if the machine issued a ticket in return – except that that, I suppose, if the railway system is any guide, would involve another machine to take the ticket away again in exchange for a bigger one, and so on. . . . The machine in fact does nothing in return for the money except to make a thin tinkling or rattling noise, yet it is a constant worry to the driver, who has repeatedly to wind a handle attached to it without producing any visible result. He has also to sort out the money which the machine from time to time disgorges into a receptacle, and stack the coins in racks in front of him. As a mathematician I am naturally interested to know what the machine is for, how it works and so on, but the drivers I have so far asked have been too busy steering with one hand and winding and stacking with the other to make any very detailed reply. One of them indeed spoke to me with some discourtesy, not realizing I dare say that I was an Englishman.

These are just a few of my first impressions of America. Of course I realize that the same points may have been noted by previous visitors to this great continent; but then if we were all careful never to say anything that had been said before there would be some pretty long silences, as I remember my Headmaster saying once apropos the end-of-term reports.

Another odd thing is that the letter-boxes on the sidewalks (one soon picks up the lingo here) are not very easy to distinguish from the rubbish bins. I pointed this out to a policeman ('cop', eh?), who reprimanded me for posting a piece of chewing gum that had somehow got stuck to my shoe, and he said, 'Is that a fact?' in a surprised tone of voice, which only shows that it takes a fresh eye to see what is going on under your own nose. 'Go ahead and drop your mail in the trash-can,' he told me. 'Just to square things up.' We both laughed at that, and I really began to feel at home in this extraordinary country. I said I had met one or two fellow-countrymen of his during the war, and he seemed very interested, telling me in return that his wife once had a canary she bought from an English lady. One lives and learns. I must say he did not seem at all the type of man to take bribes or hit people on the head with rubber hosepipes.

I was standing in front of a shop on Fifth Avenue, reading an advertisement that said 'Not Just Leisure Togs . . . *but* Star Studded Groups of *Newsmaking Sportswear*' and thinking for some reason of Oliver Wendell Holmes, when a total stranger came up and addressed me.

'How's it go then?' he said. 'How d'you find it?'

'Find it?' I asked.

'All this,' he said. 'New York. Different to London, eh?'

'Yes, indeed. Yes. Oh yes. Different from London certainly,' I agreed, taking care not to stress the corrected preposition. 'Rather!'

At home I do not often say 'Rather!', but they expect it over here, so I am told.

'Well?' he said. 'Such as what? What's the impression, tell me?'

'Well,' I said, thinking back over my walk, 'your sewers steam more than ours do. Not that –'

'For God's sake!' he said.

'It comes up out of the manholes,' I told him. 'It's just a thing one notices, walking along.'

'Sanitation man?' he asked.

'Certainly not. I am a schoolmaster, as it happens.'

'I see,' he said. 'Anything else strike you?'

I told him how surprised I was to see so few men wearing hats – on Fifth Avenue, that is. They seemed to start wearing them on Fourth Avenue, and the further east you went the more there were to be seen. 'I walked down to the river, you know,' I explained, tracing the route with the point of my umbrella, and added, without thinking, that there were clumps of grass growing out of the pavement, or sidewalk, on First Avenue. 'A kind of barley, I think,' I said, hoping he would not suppose any criticism was intended.

'Is that so?' he asked, and I was about to say a tactful word about the weeds in bomb-damaged areas near St Paul's when a new voice remarked, 'Went right down to First, so he says,' and I looked up to find that quite a group had gathered to listen to our conversation. Well, really! I suppose it is natural that people should want to hear what an Englishman thinks of their country, but all the same!

'It's not much of a walk, madam,' I remarked, and told her, just to be friendly (one has to do what one can to kill the absurd canard that the English are stand-offish), that I intended to walk the other way in the afternoon, right down to Eleventh.

'I'd certainly be glad to hear your impressions after *that* trip,' the first man said.

'How so?' I asked, pricking up my ears in the hope of a few tips about items of special interest to look out for.

'Well,' he said, 'there's a devil of a lot of steam comes out of the manholes in those parts.'

There was a general laugh at this, and another when I put a question that had been bothering me since the beginning of our walk, namely just how I had been recognized as an Englishman before I had even opened my mouth. This habit of laughing for little or no reason is a form of shyness, I think. My IIIA boys back at Burgrove often break out in much the same way, when nothing funny has been said. Still, it all makes for friendliness. 'Mind you don't trip over the grass,' somebody called out when I eventually went on my way – to which I retaliated by pretending to clear a path along the sidewalk with swishes of my umbrella. I found myself humming a little tune as I strolled along, always a sign that I am enjoying myself. These informal encounters, so typical of this great country, are very warming to a stranger, and do a great deal I am sure to foster mutual understanding. I certainly intend to speak to as many Americans as I can while I am over here. It will at least prove to them, other things apart, that not all Englishmen are nincompoops with monocles.

A drawing of a cat caught my eye at what these extraordinary people call a traffic intersection. I have never cared for the use of dumb animals, pets, manikins and so on to give warning or advice; words put into the mouths of squirrels or bears seem to me to lose rather than gain authority. So that I was somewhat shocked to read, in the very heart of what we must now regard as the capital of the Western world, the legend

'Tweets' says HEY! that light's gonna change.
Cross at the start of the green, not in between

'This is worse than the Whispering Fish,' I remarked to a bystander in overalls, momentarily forgetting that he would not in all probability be familiar with the advertisements issued some time ago by our own White Fish Authority. He looked nonplussed and put a hand up to the back of his curious cap, which had flaps, I noticed, buttoned up at the sides. 'It gives recipes for cod and so on,' I explained. 'In a kind of balloon.' The fish has a fin up to its mouth, actually, to show that it is whispering, and I was trying to make this clear when the lights changed and the man rapidly crossed the street, as instructed, at the start of the green. Americans are surprisingly law-abiding in many ways, which is a good thing I suppose; but it is disconcerting when they move off suddenly before you have made your point clear.

I did not get to Eleventh actually, as there was a message

at my hotel from Mr Bulkin, asking me to call him back. It looks as though the more serious side of my trip is about to begin.

A Lecture

Judging by my experience so far, the lectures I came over here to give – lecture, rather, for of course the actual talk will be the same though the audiences, I suppose, will differ – seem likely to arouse a certain amount of interest. A surprising number of women appear to want to know about English educational theory, and I shall do my best to oblige them, though the only theory worth tuppence in my experience is that if you say a thing fifty thousand times three boys out of ten may remember it. From the questions some of these ladies asked at the end of my talk yesterday I doubt very much whether they have ever taught geometry to a roomful of twelve-year-olds on a warm July afternoon.

'Does the lecturer not agree that infinite care and tenderness should be exercised to secure the willing cooperation of those young personalities that find difficulty in canalizing their enthusiasms to fit a perhaps all-too-rigid syllabus?'

A woman in a purple hat put this question to me yesterday, and to save time I said that I agreed; but I confess that I rather lost patience when she went on to ask whether it was not of vital importance, when budding minds were reaching out eagerly after knowledge, to avoid the risk of overstrain.

'Madam,' I said, 'I have been teaching mathematics to budding minds for thirty-five years and never had a case of overstrain yet.'

One would have thought that that would have ended the matter, but another woman said that the damage done in the early years often showed itself only in maturity, and a third declared that she knew of a case where a very lovely personality was warped by an unchecked indulgence in trigonometry. 'The delicate membranes of the anterior lobe,' she explained, and two or three women in the audience nodded their heads in an understanding way.

I thought it was about time we all faced the facts.

'There seems to be some misconception,' I said warmly, 'about the problem of teaching small boys. The risk of doing them lasting harm is unfortunately negligible. One moment, madam, *please*. The real problem is to find out what the little devils are up to. If this gathering were my old IIIA mathematical set, instead of the Ladies Guild of – ah – Mutual Advancement and Studies, I dare say I could show you one or two things that might surprise you. The lady in the front row here with her head in her hands may or may not be suffering from overstrain; if she were one of my boys I should know she was eating toffee, a practice forbidden at Burgrove during school hours. Overstrain indeed! Allow me to tell you that when two boys follow a demonstration with frowns of concentrated attention (such as I am favoured with from the two ladies on my right), no schoolmaster worth his salt fears damage to their anterior lobes. He suspects, and rightly, that they are fencing, under cover of their desks, with school pens and endeavouring to jab each other in the fleshy part of the leg. The golden rule,' I told them, raising my voice to avoid interruption, 'is this. Never pass over a look of genuine interest. Whenever a boy has the appearance of – what was the phrase, madam? – eagerly reaching out after knowledge, make him stand up and show you what he has in his hand. The surreptitious reading of novels in the third row –'

'Who? Me! I beg your pardon,' called out a woman suddenly, blushing in rather a becoming way. 'I was only just glancing. . . .'

There was some laughter at this unexpected intervention, and a girl in front turned round to call out 'Caught you there, Mavis! Still up to the same old High School tricks.'

'Don't *you* talk, Hester,' the first woman replied. 'You and that elastic contraption of yours in the Art Class. It's a wonder poor Miss Egerton. . . .'

'Did any of you girls ever try pepper in a balloon, and then kind of let it go backwards?' asked a plumpish lady with grey hair piled on top, but several voices called out that it was old. Then quite a discussion broke out about writing messages in reverse on hand mirrors, which I could not quite follow, and in the end I had some difficulty in making myself heard.

'Ladies! Ladies!' I cried. 'We are discussing overstrain. Please make less noise or I shall have to keep the class in this afternoon.'

There was much laughter at this sally, but they quietened down, and the lady in the purple hat presently asked me whether corporal punishment was still permitted in English schools. I told her that it was very rare, I believed, in State schools, but that of course in private schools, such as Burgrove, where the formation of character. . . .

'You mean you have to pay to get it done?' interrupted a motherly-looking woman at the back. There was a wistful note in her voice which made me feel that Americans, for all their tendency to highfalutin talk, are still sound enough at heart.

Afterwards there was tea and coffee, dispensed from what looked more like silver samovars than one would expect in the heart of a great democracy. Not that we were in the heart exactly, in a geographical sense, but one knows what one means. I believe we were in New Jersey, though it is hard to be certain. In the ordinary way at home I am as sure of my whereabouts as the next man, but they have a way of ushering one into a car and driving off over here that is quite confusing. 'It's just around the corner,' Mr Bulkin said, and then to my surprise did not get into the car himself but handed me over to a woman in a red hat who addressed me as Mr Wentridge throughout and was descended from Oliver Cromwell.

'Warts and all?' I asked, without thinking, and was quite relieved when she replied that it was on the distaff side mostly. She missed that one, as Mr Schnaffler would say.

However, that is by the way. We got to wherever it was in the end, and I looked eagerly round to see what I could see. It is not every day, after all, that one has an opportunity to look over an American country community for the first time. Nothing struck me, however. A difficulty about the American countryside is that it looks rather like parts of England, only browner. One misses the foreign language signs on shops and so on that make the Continent (Europe, I mean) so different. All this will change, I have no doubt, as one goes further afield. I am not so naïve as to suppose that the whole of this great country resembles Surrey in a drought. All I mean is that so far there was not very much to get *hold* of.

I tried to explain this to Mrs Enkel, after the lecture, but she had this education bee in her bonnet and could not be diverted. She kept telling me that *visual demonstration* was so important to the developing mind, as she felt sure I would agree, as opposed to mere verbal instruction.

'I feel sure I should *not* agree, madam,' I said at last with some impatience, after the fifth repetition of the word 'plastic' for which I have no manner of use. 'If you are suggesting that I should make use of wooden isosceles triangles and introduce my boys to the properties of the circle by grinning at them through prefabricated horse-collars, I can only reply that half the difficulty with young boys is to *stop* them thinking that triangles and circles have to be 'real' to be worth bothering with. The square on the hypotenuse –'

'Oh my!' exclaimed a new voice. 'That old square on the hypotenuse!'

'Exactly,' I said. 'I take leave to doubt whether the Theorem of Pythagoras would become either more comprehensible or more palatable by the construction of a ridiculous triangular framework with excrescences on all three sides. Even drawing the thing on the blackboard can mislead minds that may or may not be developing. I well remember one of my boys, many years ago, actually asking me whether it was a likely thing to happen – whether, as he put it, a triangle was *likely* to have squares on all its three sides at once. "I mean in real life," he said. What nonsense! The whole point that one has to get into their thick skulls is that it does not matter two hoots –'

Suddenly becoming aware that a natural desire to emphasize this vital aspect of education had made me raise my voice and that everybody else in the room had stopped talking, I apologized for continuing my lecture beyond its appointed limits, and at once, in order to make an easy transition to ordinary social conversation, asked the first question which came into my head.

'Who runs New Jersey?' I inquired, more or less at large.

Nobody seemed to know. But a lady in a green hat said that her great-grandfather came from Inverness, to which I could not resist replying 'By way of the Cape, I suppose?' However, Americans do not seem very quick at understanding our English jokes, so I added after a little silence that the ties of kinship and a common language and so forth and so on that bound our two countries together could never, I was convinced, be broken. 'I don't believe a little difference of opinion about the best way of teaching the Theorem of Pythagoras,' I said with a laugh, 'is going to keep us apart.'

After that, somebody asked me, as usual, for my impressions of the country – they need constant reassurance, I suppose – and I said that it was early days yet, but seeing so many books by English authors in their bookshops made me feel very much at home. I was going on to say a good word for some T-bone steak I had very much enjoyed in New York, for I am determined to lose no chance of playing the good ambassador, when one of my little knot of – well, fans almost, exclaimed that my cup was empty, as indeed it was.

'There's visual demonstration for you, Mrs Enkel,' I said with a twinkle; and could not resist adding that if I had had recourse to old-fashioned verbal methods my cup would have been refilled ten minutes ago. 'Not that I really wanted another,' I said, to soften it.

One way and another the time passed all too quickly, and when I said goodbye to the president I told her how touched I had been by the reception given to an unknown stranger in a very strange land.

'Unknown, Mr Wentworth!' she protested. 'Your name will be a legend here. You will never be forgotten.'

I confess that the warm-heartedness of these people is sometimes almost too much for my composure.

A Trip to the Rockies

I sent a picture postcard to Gilbert, showing the Rockies as viewed from Denver – really a very fine spectacle with which we have nothing to compare – but it was not easy. One looks in vain in an American hotel for the kind of head porter who makes everything so simple in, say, Switzerland. There are plenty of officials about, some of them behind bars as in banks, but most of them are always dealing with something else, and if you try to question one of them about bus time-tables and where to get English tobacco and the best way to send a box of sweets to Mrs Butterhouse at 549B Westway Drive, you will be lucky to get more than a jerk of the thumb in the direction of some other attendant who does nothing but cash traveller's cheques and tells you so. Naturally, before buying a stamp, I wanted to know what sort of stamp to put on a postcard to England, but the man I asked about that seemed to specialize in cablegrams and pointed to a kind of bookstall where the woman in charge said she only *sold* stamps; she didn't aim to know about rates and schedules and such. She sent me back to the cablegram man who directed me, or so I thought from his thumb, to a smallish uniformed man, who gave me a comparatively friendly wink when I said I wanted to send a postcard to England.

'My elevator don't go sideways,' he told me. 'She only goes up.' I enjoy a good laugh at my own expense as much as the next man, but, really, to be sent scurrying to and fro in this ridiculous way under the eyes of a row of motionless men with their hats on, who seem to sit about all day in the lobbies of Colorado hotels doing absolutely nothing, was beyond a joke. I suppose they are ranchers who like to watch people instead of cows once in a while. They have long, wrinkled, impassive faces, and wear boots with sloping heels under their thin pale trousers. In any properly-run hotel in my country somebody would very soon ask them their business and send them about it in short order. However, one must accept things as they are, remembering that it will be all the same in a hundred years.

Certainly, it was all the same next morning. There they were, ranged all along the wall, as if they had been sitting there all night just to see whether I should catch my heel again coming out of the elevator. I had half a mind to pretend to mistake them for messenger boys and ask one of them, quite politely of course, to take a box of sweets to 549B Westway Drive. It must be a devil of a long walk, if one starts at the wrong end. That is by the way, though. I got my card off to Gilbert eventually, after being sent from pillar to post – or rather to anywhere *but* post – to tell him that it was heigh-ho for the Rocky Mountains in the morning and mail could be sent to me care of the post office in Santa Fe, unless I had an urgent call from Mr Bulkin to go to Boston instead. Santa Fe is not in the Rockies, naturally, but one has to think ahead as far as is possible when one is not quite sure where one is going.

How to describe the grandeur of America's most notable range? I am not much of a hand at that kind of thing, but I jotted down some notes as we went along, which may be of interest to stay-at-homes.

9.24 a.m. Entered first tunnel, 100 yards long. (I made a note of thirty-one tunnels in all, on the way to the top, putting down the length of each for my boys. They will enjoy adding them together and so on.)

9.31 Looked down from the Vistadome, which is a kind of greenhouse on top of the coach, and spotted another train coming up just below, where the track bends round on itself. It seemed dangerously close, until I realized it was the back end of our own train. There is no keeping up with these Americans. Nobody else in the world would think of hauling so long a train up a place like this. We have two engines, of course, but even so!

9.40 Playing on my braces as on a zither – American millionaire. (One's notes are not always quite clear after a lapse of time. I like to jot down snatches of conversation which seem characteristic, and this must be one of them, I think. All the same, it is rather a puzzle.)

9.43 Fine views backwards.

9.26 Sixteenth tunnel. 800 yards. (Here again one does not quite know. The timing is unmistakable in my notes and is confirmed by the following entry: '9.28 Nobody about. Query too high?' My maths set will be after me like a pack of hounds if I tell them I have been through sixteen tunnels in minus two minutes. Mountain Time could make a difference, of course, if I remembered to put my watch back or forward as the case may be. One has to be on the *qui vive* out here, and no mistake!)

There is nothing else of general interest in my notes until 10.19, which seems rather early in the day to have reached a height of 9,000 feet and should perhaps read 11.19. The Moffat Tunnel is 6.2 miles long and gave rise to a short conversation in which I fancy I gave as good as I got. 'Used to be the longest railroad tunnel in the western hemisphere,' my neighbour told me, quoting as I happened to know from the brochure kindly issued by the Denver and Rio Grande Western Railroad company. 'You don't have anything like this in your country, I guess.'

'No,' I agreed. 'No, we haven't.' And I added that our engineers, when planning our railways, had gone out of their way to avoid obstructions over six miles wide.

'They'd have had to go a mighty long way out of their way to avoid this one,' he said. 'Maybe a thousand miles, give or take a few hundred.'

'That may well be so,' I began.

'No maybe about it,' he said. 'This is a big country.'

'Of that I am well aware, sir,' I replied, without raising my voice. 'I merely wished to point out that even in my small island there are mountain ranges in which it would be possible to bore tunnels six or seven or even ten miles long, should anyone wish to take the trouble to do so.'

'God dammit to hell,' he exclaimed, without I am sure intending any irreverence.

I see that I had a sandwich in the Silver Chalet at 11.25, which I think must indicate a break in our conversation. We have no Silver Chalets on our English trains, as I should be the first to admit. The ham in the sandwich, however, was not as good as our York. We were by this time descending through some remarkable gorges of a red and green hue, and on returning to my seat in the Vistadome (not feasible at home owing to our low bridges) I observed to my neighbour that it was indeed a magnificent feat to have cut a railway through such a mountain range as this.

'The Colorado River cut this ditch, not us,' he said.

'Yes, yes, yes,' I said. 'What I mean is that only a race of supermen, as my boys would say, would dream of building a railway, railroad, at the bottom of so inhospitable a chasm. I am astounded.'

'Oh, come now,' he said. 'Don't tell me that if you British had thought it worth the trouble –'. He broke off there, catching a glimpse perhaps of the grin I was unable entirely to suppress, and asked me after a while where I was heading for.

'Glenwood Springs,' I told him.

'What goes on at Glenwood Springs, then?'

'I hardly know as yet,' I reminded him. 'The fact is I am really making for Santa Fe, but a Mr and Mrs Riggery are half expecting me at Colorado Springs so, not liking to take advantage of their hospitality, I thought I would make a round trip from Denver, coming back through the Royal Gorge which is one thousand and fifty three feet deep, and then slip down quietly to Santa Fe on the Aitchison, Topeka and Santa Fe. I could ring them up, you see, and explain that owing to a misunderstanding –'

'You'll be stopping off at Pueblo, of course,' he put in.

'Well, no,' I said. 'No, I don't think so. No.'

He turned to me with so incredulous a look that I felt I

had inadvertently been guilty of some kind of *gaffe*. 'What goes on at Pueblo, then?' I echoed, rather wishing I had my *World Almanack* at hand for reference.

'Pueblo,' he said, 'that's the steel city of the West. That's something you have to see. That's the biggest – there's blast furnaces there turning out a matter of three and three-quarter. . .'

'We have blast furnaces in England, you know,' I felt obliged to point out.

'Not like Pueblo you haven't,' he said.

'You know England well?' I inquired. 'You have been to Sheffield?'

When it turned out that he had not been to England and never even heard of Sheffield, I naturally wondered how he felt in a position to make comparisons. But he appeared to be not in the least disconcerted.

'You weren't ever at Pueblo,' he said. 'So we're quits on that.'

In the face of such utter illogicality, not to say insularity, I felt further argument to be useless and contented myself with gazing up at the enormous walls of Glenwood Canyon (1.22 p.m.) which give one a sensation of being, as it were, very much enclosed. The famous Grand Canyon is said to be even deeper, but that of course one looks down into from the top instead of up into from below, unless one makes the journey down by mule. 'This one is good enough for me, whichever way you look at it,' I said to myself; and insensibly I began to rehearse the descriptive phrases I might use back at Burgrove, supposing some move were made to try to persuade me to give an account of my adventures. Indeed I jotted down one or two remarks:

1.30 Whole forests cling within the folds and fissures that scar these precipices, green against red, and, unimaginably remote, the topmost crags jut out against the deep blue Colorado sky.

1.38 Clinging by the skin of its teeth to the base of the cliffs, diving into the living rock when the river grudges even that precarious foothold, emerging again to snake cautiously along beside the ever-swelling torrent, the Delaware and Rio Grande is indeed a veritable tour-de-force of engineering.

1.52 Now the great bastions roll back, and out into a green and sunlit bowl, etc., etc.

But I don't know, you know. Boys are queer cattle, and might prefer just a straight talk about the food and so on. I must think about it.

I was gathering up my traps when my neighbour suddenly spoke. 'So you have boys, eh?' he said.

'Boys,' I repeated, in some surprise, supposing that I must have spoken my thoughts aloud.

'Way back,' he said, 'you were saying your boys would say we were supermen round here.'

'Oh that,' I said. 'Boys. Well, yes, you might say I have boys, in a manner of speaking. I teach, you know.'

'Teach, is it?' he said. 'Well now! You go see Pueblo, then you'll have something to tell 'em about.'

Every country has its self-satisfied bores, I suppose. I certainly would not dream of regarding this one as in any way representative of this great and, on the whole, friendly and modest people. 'Good day to you, sir,' I said, and stepped out into the refreshing air of Glenwood Springs, where the climate (so says the brochure) is remarkably salubrious and the sunshine exhilarating.

And so they are.

Down South

One makes jottings as one goes along, though some of them are not very clear owing to people coming in, worry about bell-hops, getting my braces caught in roomette, etc. A man in a train, seeing that I was worried about tips, very kindly gave me his Weekly Expense Report form, which had a scale of tipping, printed on the back. 'Double what it says and run for your life,' he advised me – in fun I think – but I find the simplest plan is to hand everyone a quarter, and then add another if they look dissatisfied. Fifty cents is not very much, as long as one does not try to convert it into English money.

I DO NOT WANT BUCKETS OF ICE IN MY BEDROOM.

I must have scribbled that in a motel, to the best of my recollection, when I pressed a button that I thought would turn off a military band in a kind of grating and a man in shirtsleeves came and dumped about a hundredweight of ice on the dressing table. I protested that it would all be wasted, but he said, 'That's only water done up in cubes,' so I gave him a quarter, and he said there was an ice machine one floor down, if I wanted more for free. 'Day *or* night,' he said, and switched on the television on his way out. I was still reading the instructions for switching it off, when he looked in again to say, 'You're from England, so you wouldn't know. We got bonded baby sitters here, free kennels, *and* piped music right under water in the pool any time you want 'em. Tell your friends.'

Rather a change from Burgrove, I must say.

I have another note, about lobsters, which was unfortunately interrupted in the middle (more ice, eh?), and a short memo on the Grand Canyon, which I decided not to visit. The fact is I asked a hotel clerk about it, and he told me that the only time he had seen it it was full up to the brim with mist. 'Looked as flat as anywhere else, Mac,' he said, in the picturesque way of talking one soon gets accustomed to here, 'only a Goddam sight less safe to walk on.' He said I might be luckier and then again I might not, so I went to Tennessee instead, which is less of a detour.

There was some muddle over this visit, because they seemed to be expecting me to give a talk on high-level dams at Nashville, and it later turned out that Mr Bulkin who has a great many irons in the fire, had sent a hydraulic engineer to a preparatory school in Massachusetts. Still, it is all in the day's work, and everyone was most kind. In the end I stayed with a very agreeable family in a place that I will call, for sufficient reasons, Sagebush. Mrs Trevor said it was a real pleasure, and showed me a faded photograph of a seventeenth-century tombstone in a church in Northumberland, which she was determined to visit before she died. Everyone to his own pleasure, I suppose. Mr and Mrs Trevor have a bathroom each, and so have the three elder children, but the youngest has only a shower, which worried them a little in case he should develop some kind of five-year-old frustration. I could not tell how many of them had cars because of the constant coming and going, but their manners were excellent all the same, and one of them asked me very politely whether we had television in England. 'We invented it,' I said with a smile, to which he replied, 'Oh, I thought it was the Russians.' They have some odd ideas, which only shows how valuable a visit like mine can be, in clearing up misunderstandings and so on.

Two men called while I was demonstrating the way to hold a cricket bat and one of them took a photograph before I had time to put down the old brass warming-pan, which was the nearest I could get to a proper instrument. You hardly ever see a poker in this country. They were from the

Sagebush Intelligence, and asked me for an interview of all things!

'Oh, I say, look here!' I said.

'Can I quote you on that?' one of them asked, resting a notebook on his knees.

'I haven't said anything yet,' I objected in some astonishment; but he only smiled and went on to inquire whether I had any thoughts about Tennessee.

'Thoughts?' I replied. 'About Tennessee? Well, I don't know, you know. Of course, it's all very different. This lad here,' I said, putting a hand on young Wilbur's shoulder, 'thinks the Russians invented television. What are your thoughts about *that*, eh?'

'Aw, gee!' the boy exclaimed.

'There you are!' I said, rubbing my hands. It was the first time I had heard anyone say 'Gee!' actually, though of course one hears 'Sure' and 'I guess' quite frequently.

'There you are, what?' Wilbur asked, and when I had explained, wanted to know what was wrong with it.

'Nothing,' I said. 'It's American, that's all. Just as all of you have been hoping to hear me say "Jolly good show!" and I haven't. Come, now. Aren't you all disappointed to find that I don't talk "silly ass" English?'

'Oh, I don't know, you know,' the reporter said.

The shot went home all the same, I think, and to make up for it I did my best to answer his questions, within reason. I had been much impressed on the way down, I told him, by the number of trees and so on, and much preferred sleeping in the same direction as the train, as one does in a roomette, rather than sideways on as in an English sleeper. 'Yours is a large country, sir,' I said warmly. 'If I had travelled as far at home I should have reached – why, God bless my soul, I should be somewhere north of the Shetland Islands, I shouldn't wonder.'

'Is that so?' he said.

'Oh yes indeed,' I said. 'And you may quote me on that.'

There was a general laugh, in which I readily joined, though to tell the truth I had not intended a joke. There are different shades and *nuances* of humour, no doubt, as it is understood in Tennessee and, say, Warwickshire. It all adds to the fun, in a way.

'We are not ashamed of being such a small country,' I told them firmly, 'any more than you are ashamed of being so large – isn't that so, Mrs Trevor?' I called out, as she appeared in the doorway with coffee.

'Oh, but I *am*, Mr Wentworth,' she said. 'That's why I never touch candy or *any*thing.'

'My dear Mrs Trevor,' I began, turning scarlet with embarrassment and distress. 'I assure you I never – I happened to be talking of my own tiny country –'

'And naturally the contrast struck you when I came into the room,' she interrupted with a smile. 'Ah well. At least I am practically on the map.'

I gave it up, and with a gesture of despair turned to look out of the window – double-glazed of course and commanding a fine view of the distant Smoky Mountains. I was deeply mortified that she should think me capable of rudeness – and in front of two newspapermen to boot. One does not come thousands of miles to be gratuitously insulting to one's hostess. I was feeling for my pipe, as I generally do in moments of anger or dismay – not that such occasions often come my way, I am happy to say – when I felt a touch on my arm, and there was Mrs Trevor offering me a cup of coffee.

'No sugar, thank you,' I said stiffly.

'You mustn't mind my pulling your leg, Mr Wentworth. I do it to all my friends, I'm afraid.' Actually she said 'mah friends' I suppose, but I was in no mood to make fine distinctions.

'I see,' I said. 'Well –'

'I just love the English,' she added softly. 'You are so mature and so – well – sort of *civilized*.'

One really cannot help feeling an affection for these extraordinary people.

'We shall grow up one day, you know,' Mrs Trevor said, and I nodded understandingly to show that I could take a bit of ribbing as well as the next man. All the same, one can't help wondering how the interview will turn out in cold print. Reporters are not always as discreet as could be wished.

One must do in Rome and the rest of it, naturally, but a triple tier of pancakes with blueberries in them, the whole thing drenched in maple syrup and with a slice of green bacon on top, is a far cry from the kind of breakfast I am accustomed to at Burgrove. 'Like it?' Mr Grew asked me, as we faced each other in the restaurant of a motel in the Smoky Mountains, and he looked so eager for my approval that I hadn't the heart to stop eating. It is quite a surprise to find myself in this beautiful National Park, except that nothing surprises me very much now. Mr Grew simply called for me at Mrs Trevor's house, apparently at her suggestion, and drove me here in his car, though I was all packed up and ready to go by coach to Richmond (Va.) At home of course one might be rather vexed at finding oneself in the Lake District, say, after intending to go to Tewkesbury, but here one might as well be in one place as another, luckily. After all, as I keep reminding myself, I am really supposed to be in Massachusetts.

There are black bears in the woods, which the brochure says are dangerous, but Mr Grew says they walk up to you quite quietly and beg for food. 'It's only when you stop feeding them that they may turn nasty,' he told me.

'What do you do then?' I asked.

'Give them some more,' he replied.

'I see,' I said. 'What happens when you run out?'

'Ah,' he said. 'That's when it gets awkward. They're just like anybody else, see? Once you start doing people favours you've got to keep right on doing it, if you don't want to get one hell of a big wallop when you stop. Am I right?'

'That's certainly true of boys, Mr Grew,' I said, laughing. And I told him of the time when, as a very young master, I made the mistake of giving out sweets for neatness.

'Set about you, did they?' he asked – a remark that made me wonder whether the standards of discipline at school were not a good deal lower in his country than in mine. Set about me, indeed!

After breakfast we looked at a copy of the *Sagebush Intelligence*, kindly sent on to me by Mrs Trevor, and I was annoyed to see that, in the photograph, my coat had somehow got hitched up on the handle of the warming-pan, giving an untidy effect. The caption, which read

Mr Wentworth, of England, currently stopping over with Mr and Mrs (at right) Stephen R. Trevor, shows how the battle of Waterloo was won with anything that came handy

simply struck me as facetious journalism at its worst. One does not mind for oneself – I am used to misrepresentation by this time, I should hope, in whichever hemisphere – but this was scarcely the kind of jocularity my good hostess would be likely to relish. At least – no.

'Wentworth of England,' quoted Mr Grew musingly. 'That has kind of a ring about it, I guess.'

'Let's go and tackle some black bears,' I said briskly, rising to my feet. There is a kind of sparkle in the air hereabouts that makes one feel half one's age and ready for anything.

In the end, though, we went to the Cherokee Reservation, where I bought a pair of moccasins. On a sudden inspiration I asked the chief in the shop (rather disappointingly dressed, I thought) whether they had special films in the Reservation. 'You know, different,' I explained. 'Cavalryman bites dust, eh?' But he only made a gesture and looked inscrutably into the distance.

'Great Red Chief he say "Not good box-office!"' Mr Grew interpreted, when we got outside. 'What do you say we find a Ten-Pin Alley and have a change from all this raw Nature?'

'O.K. Mac,' I said gaily. 'Let them roll.'

Later, while we were eating broiled whole gulf flounder with hush puppies, and blueberry cobbler to follow, I remember thinking that I should have plenty to tell the boys about when I got home. And tomorrow as ever is I am off to Williamsburg, via Richmond (Va.), on Mr Grew's advice. 'It's good for a laugh any day,' he told me. He has been a most pleasant companion, but like many Americans can be a little cryptic at times.

Come Again, and Stay Longer

It has all been rather a whirl, but I think it was at a place called Ashville that I was taken to a tobacco auction, where the noise was quite deafening and a man kept writing figures on scraps of paper, which he then threw over his shoulder as if they were useless. I was reminded, for some reason, of my mathematics set at home. Tobacco is sold in surprisingly small heaps for so large a country and I wanted to ask my guide about this but it was time to catch my coach to Raleigh, so I shall have to look it up in Mr Gunther's book. There is much to learn.

My coach went very fast and I was unable to make notes about the countryside, but we stopped for thirty minutes at a restaurant (they sound the final 't' here, but leave out the second 'l' in a word like travelled, or 'traveled' rather, which seems curious). A girl at the counter told me, in answer to my inquiry (*in*quiry', not 'in*quiry*'; though there again they say 'prim*ar*ily' instead of '*prim*arily', so that one hardly knows whether one is on one's head ('on *his* head', they would say, even if it was a woman!) or her heels – anyway, this girl said 'A barbecue sandwich is a barbecue sandwich, and that's all I can say.' Really! Americans are not generally so tongue-tied by any means. I scored off her by replying that if a cup of tea was a cup of tea I would have that instead. But it turned out, when I took a sip of it, not to be. Land of contrasts, eh?

Some jottings I made about the rest of my trip may help to give an idea of the pace of life in this country.

Thursday. To Richmond (Va.), where I visited the State Capitol and the Confederate Museum. They are more interested here in the Civil War than in, say, the War of Independence, which seems a little insular, though of course I was careful not to say so. However, I did remark to the agreeable lady who showed me General Robert E. Lee's sword and so forth that in my country we preferred to remember our victories over our enemies rather than defeats by our own countrymen, to which she replied, 'Is that so?' with an intonation that I shall hope to bear in mind in case Mason and the others should ever get a bit above themselves. Gunther says that the Byrd machine runs Virginia, but when I inquired about it I was told that Byrd flew it to the South Pole. Or perhaps the North. In either case it hardly seems to fit in.

Friday. A quick trip to Williamsburg, kindly arranged for me by a man named Smollett who is no relation, he tells me. Very impressive and quite old, though much of it was only built recently. The Union Flag was flying at the Magazine and I found myself a good deal moved. 'Let it roll,' as Churchill said. A silversmith in one of the craft shops recognized me as British, perhaps because my cap has no flaps at the sides, and told me that one gramme of silver can be drawn out to a length of one mile, cold. Fancy! I bought a bracelet for three dollars, thinking that Myra Fitch might find some use for it, but declined 'melted fnappy cheefe' at the ancient tavern. 'Melted cheefe is Welfh Rarebit, and that's all I can say,' I said jokingly to the waiter, who seemed to be at a loss and made a rejoinder that came strangely from the lips of a man dressed like Doctor Johnson. Still, it is all good fun. To round the thing off I ordered 'Pecan Wassles', pretending to think the double 'f' stood for two 's's, and went off in high good humour to see the House of Burgesses, where Patrick Henry said 'If this be treason, make the most of it.' Which they did, of course; but that is all forgiven and forgotten now.

Unlike the Civil War, I might add.

Saturday. Found the key of my room at Raleigh still in my pocket when getting ready to leave the John Marshall Hotel at Richmond. American hotels very sensibly have addressed labels attached, ready for posting in such cases, so I slipped the key into the mail box – only to find that I had posted the John Marshall key by mistake. The two were rather alike, I suppose, which would account for it. It seemed best to leave the Raleigh key quietly on the counter, to even things up, and get along without fuss to Boston, where I have a fullish programme in store for me – thanks to Mr Bulkin, who has worked indefatigably to get me to the right place at the right time and thinks he has pulled it off at last.

I find I am staying with a Mr Gee, who is a friend of a friend of some people I should have met in Philadelphia had I gone there as was originally planned. He gave me tea, which might well have been thrown into the harbour, and later on taught me how to eat clams. One pulls off a kind of small black stocking before dipping the residue in clam juice and butter. Interesting. To bed, rather tired, after a long talk about vegetables.

Sunday. Massachusetts is said to be very 'English', and certainly it is full of East Anglian names, reminders of British defeats, etc., etc. They think a great deal of Paul Revere, whom I must remember to look up. Americans come to England to see where their ancestors were born, and I suppose it is only fair, on our return visits, that they should show us where our ancestors were killed. Mrs Gee, when I remarked on this, told me that I certainly had a most interesting and well-rounded personality, which left me a little at a loss. Not for the first time in this country, surprisingly enough. Mr Gee has arranged for me to visit a college and a school, but I am taking the news with a pinch of salt. Over here, when they say 'at school' they sometimes mean what we should call 'at the university', and vice versa, up to a point. Time will show.

We went out to dinner at somebody's house in Cambridge (Mass., of course), and a great many people were drinking whisky, in which I joined. However it turned out to be not the house but another at which we had just called in *en route*. A Miss Trincham made fun of my waistcoat, and I sat in a car with three Harvard professors, which made me laugh. Afterwards there was a garden path, full of uphill bits and hollows, and I sat on the floor and ate half a leg. 'Half a leg, half a leg, half a leg onwards!' I told them, entering into the spirit of the thing, but when we got home I remembered I had forgotten to say goodbye to my hostess and wanted to go back. Gee said it had been a long day, so I went to bed, to humour him. Of course, I didn't know who she was; otherwise I might have insisted. 'I am a kind of ambassador,' I reminded him, and he agreed.

Monday. Smith College turned out to be a university for women, not a boys preparatory school at all. A very different kettle of fish from Burgrove in a number of respects. So I put my notes on the teaching of elementary mathematics, on which I had half expected to give a talk, back in my pocket and had a general look round. Everybody very kind, as usual. Six girls gave me coffee from a very fine silver set. They introduced me to an older woman, who I understood to be their 'House Mother' and seemed to be there as a sort of chaperone. At *my* age! 'Somebody has cried "Wolf! Wolf!" once too often,' I remarked with a smile, to get things going; but our allusive British fun is sometimes a bit too much for these Americans, and I very soon turned to more serious topics. I spoke of the English way of life, mentioning cricket, primroses and so forth, and in return one of the girls asked me whether it was true that our towel-rails were heated. Nothing but good can come of such exchanges, it seems to me.

The Dean very kindly gave me some booklets about Smith College, from which I learned that there are 422,000 books in the library and no fewer than 147 Doctors of Philosophy on the Faculty, as it is called; unless, of course, I counted some of the names twice over. It is all a very far cry from Burgrove.

Tuesday. And now I *am* at a boys 'Preparatory School' named after one of the Apostles, but it is actually what we should call a Public School except that they play ice-hockey in the winter, which we of course do not on account of the Gulf Stream. Some of the senior boys came into the Headmaster's study in the evening to smoke a cigarette with him, but I said nothing, remembering that at Eton and Westminster and so on beer used to be drunk at breakfast in the old days. Otherwise, it was all so like any school at home that the tears came into my eyes during the hymn in Chapel, particularly as singing obscures the American accent to some extent.

'It all seems a great pity,' I observed to the Headmaster afterwards; but I declined to elaborate when he asked me to explain, and turned the talk to crumpets instead, which we had had, to my astonishment, at tea. One of the staff asked me what was the purpose of my visit to the States, and, while I was pondering my reply, added, 'Well, put it another way. Have you achieved it, whatever it was?'

'Oh yes, indeed!' I said warmly.

'Then you must know what it was,' he rejoined.

'Oh very well,' I said, giving the Headmaster a wink to show that I was not in earnest. 'It was to find out whether you are a fit people to assume the leadership of the Western world.'

'And are we?' he pursued, apparently in a serious vein.

'I think so,' I said, and told him of a notice I had seen at Smith College, advertising a Folksong Concert, which read (as well as I could remember)

Sponsored by the Hampshire – Franklin Committee for a Sane Nuclear Policy and the Pioneer Valley Folklore Society

'What does that prove?' he asked.

'It proves that you are as muddle-headed as we are,' I told him, amid general laughter. He seemed dissatisfied, however; and so, when I thought things over in bed, was I. In a way. What *am* I here for? It is high time I found out really, since tomorrow it is heigh-ho for New York and the last farewells.

Still, whatever it is, I have enjoyed it.

Last Day. I was still a little worried the next morning and asked Mr Bulkin, who very kindly met me at the airport, straight out, 'What am I here for?', but he took the question too literally, as Americans sometimes do, and said I was there to give a talk to the Ladies Guild of Mutual Advancement and Studies – which I could hardly believe since I had already addressed them over a fortnight ago. When I explained that all my arrangements were made to return to England by air that night he said he was gosh-darned if he knew where the days got to, and we must have a farewell party. He is a most likeable and ebullient sort of man, with a fund of good will, but he reminds me at times of dear old Poole, who was put in charge of drawing up the School time-table for a brief period and had the Lower Fourth down to take three different subjects in three different classrooms at the same time in the afternoon – and on a half-holiday at that!

Wondered whether to go to the Metropolitan Museum of Art, but I remembered I had one or two little things to buy. Rested afterwards. Shopping here is on rather a bigger scale than the General Store in Fenport and takes it out of one, I find. There is a kind of brusqueness among bus conductors, shop assistants and minor officials of one sort or another that the visitor finds disconcerting, though they mean well. I remember a thing in Denver that I don't think I put down at the time. It came to mind while I was resting in Central Park, because the Natural History Museum which I was anxious to see was also in the Park (in Denver City Park, that is) so that one thing suggested another. The Park has elk, eagles and so on in it (I am not talking about *Central* Park, naturally, though that has them too, actually), and there was baseball practice going on against a background of the Rocky Mountains, which made me feel momentarily very far from home. Another foreign thing I noticed was that trees in America seem to hold their branches up at an angle well above the horizontal, whereas in our country they either droop or, as with oaks, stick out at about ninety degrees: a curious circumstance not mentioned, I think, by

Gunther. There was also a statue of a grizzly bear with an inscription on the base which I copied down there and then, thinking it might be of interest to the boys. So often it is only afterwards that one wishes one had taken the trouble to jot down whatever it may be; and then of course it is too late.

So that, what with one thing and another, it was close on half-past four before I entered the Museum, but even so I was a good deal chagrined to be brusquely informed 'Closing in a couple of minutes' by an official at the entrance.

'Oh, look here!' I said. 'You can't do that.' And I added, half-jokingly, 'You know, I have come the best part of six thousand miles to see your famous Museum.' Which was true enough, in a way.

'Should have started sooner,' was all the man said.

I took it in my stride of course, and just nodded. But I should certainly have had something to say, had the incident occurred in England. As it was, I just had time to see the Rat-tailed Skunk (stuffed, naturally) before they turned me out again, which was a disappointment. I had hoped for at least a glimpse of deer, bear, raccoons, etc., which I happen to know are hunted in Wisconsin, not far away. The point is, though, that when I left the official remembered me and gave me a friendly grin.

'Come again,' he said ' – and stay longer!'

One can't help liking them, in the long run.

I mention this by the way and to fill in time, so to speak, while I was resting in the Park – *Central* Park. Soon after that it was time to go along to Mr Bulkin's party, where I was welcomed with characteristic warmth by a Mr Charles Pulovsky, representing my host who had gone to Seattle again. George A. Mopus was there, however, and Mrs Teeling and old Schnaffler and Mrs Enkel, over specially from New Jersey, and a very pleasant couple who said they would never forgive me for not looking them up in Chicago when I was there. 'But I never was!' I cried, shaking hands with Fergus Henson Jr., who had just been de-hospitalized, he told me, and introduced me in turn to a petite lady, rather like Miss Stephens, from down South.

'Meet the Man Who Never Was,' he told her gaily. 'Mr Wentworth, from England.'

'Mr *Went*worth!' she cried, and insisted on giving me a hug, saying that it came from Mrs Trevor, by express from Tennessee. 'And that's from me,' she added. Half America, it seemed to me, had come to say goodbye, though that's exaggerating of course, or had sent messages by their friends, and I caught myself looking round to see whether Mr and Mrs Riggery had come up from Colorado Springs. They all crowded round, asking me about their country, of which they seem to know surprisingly little, and I told them as best I could what I had seen and done.

'Your great country has opened my eyes in no uncertain terms,' I said. 'Whoa, Mr Pulovsky. Thank you. I raises my glass, likewise I nods. I have been particularly impressed by your young womanhood – notably in Tennessee,' I added with a slight bow which was rather absurdly acknowledged by Mr Schnaffler. 'And of course by the Moffat Tunnel, which is 6·2 miles long from end to end. What else have I seen? Mr Pulovsky, you are extremely kind and good, but really! Your broiled tenderloin steak I shall always remember, but bacon and blueberries with maple syrup is, if you will forgive me, an acquired taste. "You can't teach an old dog new tricks", as I said to the attendant when I caught my braces in a roomette and missed the Royal Gorge in consequence. We have nothing of the kind in my country, nothing at all.'

'Blueberries or roomettes?' somebody asked.

'Way down South,' I began, putting my glass on the floor in order to make a wide gesture, only to find that I had another one in my left hand, 'I was privileged – Mrs Teeling, I am so sorry. You are drenched. Naturally, as a schoolmaster, I took a particular interest in the young wherever I went. But they don't seem to ride bicycles. Why so few bicycles, eh, Mopus?'

'Isn't he a pet?' said a woman with rather a high red hat.

This absurd interpolation momentarily made me lose my

thread and, as time was getting on, I put on my own hat and told them about my encounter at the Denver Museum. After that, we talked of a good many things and it was all I could do to avoid eating the clam patties that young Henson kept handing round. 'When I get back to Burgrove I shall tell my boys all about you dear, kind people,' I said to them seriously. They were pleased, I think, and patted me on the back, which is not a thing I encourage in the ordinary way. Still, everything is different over here, as I said many times to Mr Pulovsky. Then it was time to go, and they all crowded round my taxi and shook me by the hand.

'Come again,' they shouted, 'and stay longer.'

I was too much moved to say more than 'God bless you all!' – and of that I managed to get out only the first word before my driver started off at high speed and threw me over backwards on to the seat. Still, it was a smiling farewell.

Home, Wentworth, eh?

I was reminded for some reason, as my aeroplane climbed up through the clouds above the airport – no dummy engines on *this* one, I hope – of a little incident in New York during my first visit (or 'stopover' as they quaintly say). An American, to whom I happened to make a remark about the Empire State Building, advised me to go up it and look down if I was so disappointed with looking up at it from below. He said even the longest cars looked like toys from up there. He also told me how many minutes it would take me to reach the ground if I cared to throw myself over. He said he would be interested to make a check-up. Americans are oddly touchy at times. However, I took his advice and found that the cars and buses on Fifth Avenue really do look like toys from a height of something over a thousand feet. All the same, I do not agree that the people look like ants, which he had also maintained. They simply look like people a thousand feet down below. Ants, after all, would be invisible from such a height.

And now here I am, as the Captain has just told us, a

good eighteen thousand feet above the Atlantic!

'From up here,' I observed to a Mr Pullinger of Minneapolis, who was sitting beside me, 'your Empire State Building would look like a needle in a haystack, what?' It was said in fun, naturally. But he was asleep. I think. Otherwise I might have brought up another small point that bothered me. They say that the top of the building sways twenty or thirty feet in a high wind, which means, I suppose, that the lift shaft is bent. It is hardly, one would have thought, a thing to boast about.

I must try to work out a problem of some sort from all these measurements, to interest my IIIA boys. And then there's this business of the sun rising at almost twice its usual speed as we fly towards it. That ought to make them think – if only I can keep awake to see it . . .

Mission Completed

No Ordinary American

'What are you doing up there, Wentworth?'

I leaned over and looked down at the Headmaster in no very equable frame of mind. There is a tone of voice in which one sometimes finds it necessary to speak to boys that should never be adopted when addressing a colleague. And quite apart from that, there have already been one or two incidents since luncheon that would have ruffled a less experienced man.

'You had better come down at once,' he shouted. 'I am expecting old Horsefeathers at three.'

It was news to me that I had anything to say to the Headmaster of our rival prep school Fox House (whose name, as it happens, is Maresdown and who has a right, fusspot though he may be, to be called by it) and I made no bones about pointing this out. 'I can hardly suppose,' I said, keeping my voice as colourless as the circumstances allowed, 'that it is I he is coming to see.'

'Probably not,' the Headmaster replied. 'All the same, if he does see you I should prefer that you were not clinging to a chimney stack at the time, with your shirt-tails hanging out. And what is that thing round your left leg? What are you *up* to, Wentworth?'

I was now seriously annoyed, and might have spoken in terms that both of us would have had cause to regret, had not Raikes started up the motor mower at that instant and made ordinary conversation almost impossible. 'Gratitude,' I was beginning to say, 'I have long ago ceased to expect,' when the hideous racket broke out below me and I wisely gave up the attempt. Taking my right hand from the stack to make a dismissive gesture, I slipped rather than rolled down the sloping roof into a kind of gulley between two gables which was surprisingly full of decayed leaves, I remember thinking, for the time of year. Had I broken a leg I should have had the Headmaster to thank for it. It is the height of folly to distract the attention of a man who is carrying out a difficult job.

However, there is no sense in crying over spilt milk – still less when, as in this case, little or no milk has actually been spilled. It is true that the length of wire which had somehow entangled itself round my leg had, in the course of my fall, pulled the television aerial askew; but the aerial was incorrectly positioned in the first place, otherwise I should never have gone up to attend to it. It is not likely, as I told the Headmaster when I reached the bottom of the fire escape, that I should crawl about on the tiles at my age, unless something were seriously wrong. All the cows and sheep were double, in addition to a good deal of distortion of their udders and so on, which made it difficult to follow what was going on and started the boys laughing in a rather unhealthy way. I am no great believer in all these modern aids to education, and it passes my comprehension what the management of a dairy herd in Suffolk has to do with us here at Burgrove. Nevertheless, if we are to prepare ourselves for the battle of life by looking at pictures of cows being electrically milked('Like a woman having a permanent wave upside-down,' as Mason had the impertinence to remark, before I could check him), it is as well that they should be clearly defined.

'Yes, yes, yes,' the Headmaster said. 'But we have men about the place, more accustomed to scrambling about at dangerous heights, who can see to these things. I really cannot have my staff . . .'

'God bless my soul!' I cried. 'A man who has been up the Rockies is not likely to make a fuss over a tupenny-ha'penny little climb . . .'

'Your suspenders have come loose,' he told me.

How typical, I thought to myself, as I strode away. When one has only recently returned from a very considerable tour up and down the United States, taking the rough with the smooth and grappling not unsuccessfully with every difficulty as it arose, it is really too much to be treated as though one were incompetent (as though *he* were incompetent, I almost wrote – not that anybody here would follow what I was after, any more than the Headmaster realizes that suspenders are braces on the other side, though not of course vice versa); as though one were incompetent, I was saying, to handle the petty contretemps of life at an English preparatory school. Nobody has any idea. Not that one expects, naturally, to be greeted as some kind of hero, or pioneer. I make no such claim. A sense of proportion is all I ask.

People who will not listen will never learn. 'Do you mean to tell me,' Gilbert asked after I had made a passing reference to a slight slip-up by Mr Bulkin, 'that they employed a man specially to send you to the wrong place? You always used to be able to manage that on your own.'

'You simply have no conception,' I returned coolly, 'of the distances involved. From Massachusetts to Tennessee, to take a single instance –'

'Oh, I see,' he said. 'If it's only an error of a hundred miles or so, you can do it by yourself. But to get you a thousand miles out of your way takes two of you. Is that it?'

'You will forgive me, Gilbert,' I said, 'if I find your humour a little thin after some of the really witty remarks, or wisecracks as they call them over there, that I have been privileged to hear. When I was in Denver, Colorado –'

'Oh, not again!' said one of my younger colleagues, coming into the Common Room in his rather over-confident way.

'Be quiet, Raikes,' Gilbert said. 'Don't you realize that Denver, which has a population twice as big as Bournemouth and exports grizzly bear hides to Portugal, is four times as far from Tuscaloosa, to take a single instance, as Burgrove is from wherever it was A.J. got to that time he set off for Cambridge? To the West rise the peaks of the ten-gallon hats –'

I left them to it, with a feeling of despair. The boys at least show more interest, though they sometimes get hold of the wrong end of the stick, and ply me with questions at times when we should, perhaps, be concentrating on irrational numbers. Still, I am a great believer in a broad general education, and they will have few enough opportunities, I dare say, of getting a first-hand account of what is now, by all accounts, the greatest country in the world.

'Tell us some more about America, sir,' they beg me; and if I am in the mood I do my best. I try to give them a picture of life in the States, and to impress upon them that Americans are very like ourselves in many ways, once one has got over the differences. But it takes time and patience to rid them of the silly notion that the whole country is teeming with cowboys and spacemen.

'Did they let you see a launching-pad?' Kingsley asked me one morning.

'Five, four, three, two, one, *whoosh*!' somebody put in.

'That was quite unnecessary, Potter,' I reproved.

'Sir, it was me, sir. Potter can't count down to three even, let alone one.'

I always have a weak spot for a boy who owns up, rather than let another take the blame, so I passed over Mason's interjection in silence. And anyway, Hopgood was saying something about rockets.

'They make such a slow start you'd never think they'd get there,' he observed.

'I have sometimes felt the same thing about some of my boys,' I remarked with a twinkle.

'Jolly good, sir,' said Wrigley, as the laughter died down. 'Is it true that the cops shoot anyone who comes running out of a bank, even if he's only late for his train?'

This is the kind of nonsense one can usefully put a stop to. I told them I had not seen a shot fired in anger during the whole time I was there, and though Notting, who gets a bit above himself at times, asked 'How many in fun?' I think it impressed them. 'The sooner you realize, all of you,' I went on, 'that the ordinary American does not spend his time jumping off the roofs of trains on to the backs of galloping horses, the better. It is time some of you grew up.'

'Steady on, sir!'

'Talking of roofs, sir, is it true . . . ?'

'Sir, what's an ordinary American *like*?'

'Sir, did you meet Johnson?'

'If I *had*, Henderson,' I told him pretty sharply, 'I hope I should have had the manners to call him *President* Johnson. As for the ordinary American – was it you who asked me that question, Blake?'

'Yes, sir. I only thought –'

'What is the ordinary American *like*, eh?'

'That's it, sir.'

I ran my mind's eye rapidly over the many delightful people I had met, in one walk of life or another. Herbert S. Bulkin I dismissed as not typical. Then there was that quaint Mr Schnaffler, and Mrs Teeling with all her bangles, and that man in the train who seemed to think that Pueblo was in some way superior to Sheffield. Once, when I was coming out of a club called the Century Association, in New York, a passing stranger took me by the arm and, without introduction or any sort, said, 'Say, do you have to be over a hundred to belong to that set-up?' I recalled, too, the silversmith at Williamsburg, making a mental note to tell the boys one day about the extraordinary lengths to which a gramme of silver can be drawn out, cold; and I could not resist a chuckle as I thought of Mr Grew's jacket, which appeared to have been cut, or hacked, from a tartan horsecloth. What an experience it had all been! Those earnest women from the Mutual Advancement lot – I had given *them* something to chew over, at any rate. Risk of overstrain, my foot!

As I stood there gazing out over the playing fields, with my gown bunched up and my hands clasped behind me as is my wont when lost in thought, I could hardly credit that it was indeed I who a few short days ago had been chatting quite at my ease with a taxi driver in North Carolina who kept canaries and sang operatic snatches as we drove along.

I remember there was rather a delay as I searched for his fare because my waistcoat or vest pockets were full of cardboard packets of matches, which are free in the United States; but he turned out to be quite a philosopher and told me that time was made for slaves. I was wondering whether an exchange of taxi drivers between, say, London and New York would help our two countries to understand each other better when I happened to turn my head and became aware that the boys were waiting expectantly for me to speak.

'I am afraid I was woolgathering,' I said with a smile. 'Where was I?'

'Way down in dear old Dixie,' Mason said.

'You were going to tell us about ordinary Americans, sir.'

'Ah yes, well, exactly,' I said. 'The fact is that there *are* no ordinary Americans, Blake.'

'I see,' he said. 'Thank you very much, sir.'

One needs more time, really, to sort out one's ideas and get one's impressions into focus. 'It is all a bit of a kaleidoscope at present,' I said to the Headmaster later on, when explaining my difficulty in getting the real America across to my boys.

'Like those cows' udders you were so worried about, you mean, Wentworth?' he suggested.

It was said jokingly, of course, but I sometimes wish –. Still, it takes all sorts to make a world, as the saying goes.

The Method

'There's a brand new way of teaching maths,' somebody announced. 'It sounds super.'

'Ask my permission, if you have something to say,' I warned, whipping round from the blackboard. 'This is not a discussion group. Nor am I interested, I may as well tell you, in a lot of nonsense about counting up to two and starting again, nor in rubbishy sets –'

'Ooh, sir! Does that mean us?'

'Yes, Notting?' I said, disregarding this silly outburst. The boy had his hand up in the proper way, and I am always prepared to listen to anyone in my Set who remembers his manners.

'Sir, it isn't binary or anything, although I met a boy last hols who. . . . Well, it's this school, you see, sir, that was in the newspaper where they begin by measuring things and putting them down in books and then they work things out and everybody is interested and finds out whatever it is they want to know. Like tiles on the floor, you know, sir.'

'It's jolly useful,' Mason was good enough to add.

'Indeed!' I said. 'It is certainly revolutionary. We have been working things out and wallpapering rooms in this Set for as long as I can remember. It is news to me –'

'Not real rooms,' Notting objected. 'These boys in the paper measure their own things themselves and everything, and then they work things out from that. So it's all, well, it's all part of it, you see – not just maths, sir. *We* are *told* the size of the room, and even then it's not a room we have ever seen, so it isn't the same, sir. We just have to divide what it says into rolls, so who cares?'

'Can we do it, sir?' they all began to chorus. 'Sir, please!

We could measure the windows both ways and then multiply. . . .'

I hung my duster carefully on its hook and went to my desk. 'Measure anything you like,' I told them. 'Not now, Mason. By all means find out the dimensions of this room in your spare time. Weigh Hopgood, if Matron will lend you her scales, and write it down in a book. But just at present we are eliminating *y*, and unless you all settle down and pay attention, we shall in all probability still be eliminating *y* this afternoon instead of watching the School play Packhurst. Is that understood by all of you?'

I had hoped that would be the end of the matter, but the Headmaster stopped me with an 'Oh – Wentworth' as I was on my way to Chapel the next morning and told me that two of my IIIA boys had asked if they might measure him.

'*Measure* you, Headmaster?' I repeated in astonishment.

'I understood they wanted to put me in a book. And what is more, Wentworth, I rather gathered they had your permission to do it.'

'This is outrageous,' I replied. 'There has been a serious misunderstanding. Please leave the matter to me, Headmaster. I will deal with it at once.'

'It has already been dealt with, A.J.,' he said chuckling. 'I am five feet eight and a half inches exactly, in my socks.'

'Do you mean to tell me,' I began – but by that time we had reached the Memorial Door and, as a matter of ordinary reverence, I broke off what I had been intending to say. In his socks! Whatever next! The 42nd Psalm is one of my favourites, but I found it difficult to concentrate, even so. If the Headmaster is to remove his boots at the bidding of a couple of silly boys it seems to me that school discipline, as it used to be understood, is practically at an end. 'Why art thou cast down, O my soul? and why art thou disquieted within me?' I found myself singing. Why *not*, indeed?

It may be believed that I was in no very good mood when

I met IIIA later in the day. I do not often let boys hear the rough side of my tongue, which can be very rough indeed, as one or two Old Burgrovians have caused to remember; one has to bear in mind that eleven and twelve-year-olds are still very young and, up to a point, defenceless. Still, there are times when a good drubbing does them no harm, and this, unless I was greatly mistaken, was one of them. I purposely omitted my customary 'Good morning, boys' as I entered the room, but as luck would have it Henderson began talking almost before I had unhitched my gown from the door handle, so the implied rebuke may have gone unnoticed.

'Sir, Mr Saunders was jolly decent, sir,' he said excitedly. 'He even held a book on top of his head while I marked.'

'I was first,' put in young Wrigley, and he read out from a little booklet 'Five feet nine and a quarter, actually.'

'That was before he took his shoes off, Worm. I made him five eight and a half, sir, so if I grow one inch every year I shall only be twenty-five –'

'It's a funny thing, sir, but if you multiply the circumference of your wrist by six –'

'What have you got there, Wrigley?' I asked sharply.

'It's a notebook, sir. We've all got them.'

'Bring it to me, please.'

These little notebooks are obtainable from the Stationery Cupboard at the special price of threepence, and I could see at a glance that every boy in the room had one on his desk. Wrigley's proved to be full of figures, of which I could make neither head nor tail; but I was determined to get to the bottom of this business and put my finger on a rough diagram of a rectangle marked off in squares.

'What is this supposed to prove, Wrigley?' I demanded.

'It's the gym, sir. It shows that you can get this room into it about eleven and a half times.'

'We shoved a broom handle across the parallel bars,' Mason interrupted, 'and, sure enough, the exterior angles were equal to the interior opposite ones. It was fab.'

I gave him a look, and he had the grace to look a little

ashamed of this outburst. 'We had to measure them with string, actually,' he admitted.

Ignoring the boy altogether, often the wisest plan, I turned back to Wrigley and asked him what precisely was the use of his exercise in applied mathematics. 'In real life, which you boys are always chattering about, we are hardly likely to try to put this room into the gym eleven and a half times, are we?'

'Not exactly, no sir. At least – anyway we did try to put two pianos into the Alcove last term, didn't we, sir?'

'So?'

'So it would have been better if we'd measured them beforehand, I should have thought, sir.'

As this was precisely what I had said to Raikes at the time I found it difficult to disagree. Besides, the boys were clearly enthusiastic about what they were pleased to consider a new approach to mathematics, and enthusiasm is a commodity that any schoolmaster worth his salt is loth to discourage. If they had a craze for measuring things, well and good. Accurate measurement, after all, is the foundation of all exact science, as somebody said, or words to that effect which used to be written up in gold lettering, I remember, on the wall of the physics lab at my own old school. I saw no reason why I should not turn their measurements to account.

'Perhaps, Wrigley,' I said, taking up a piece of chalk, 'since you have obviously taken such an interest in the gymnasium, you would oblige me with its dimensions?'

'Could I have my notebook, sir?'

When I had returned the boy's notes he made a great palaver over finding the right place, complaining that he had measured Hopgood for a suit and got mixed. 'I think it's eighty-three feet six inches long,' he said at last, 'unless that's all the dining-room tables added together.'

'It's seventy-two four.'

'It's not.'

'I made it seventy-one nine,' said somebody.

'Seventy-two four will do very well,' I said, writing it up on the board to stop any further argument. 'And the width, Kingsley?'

'Well, that was a bit tricky, sir, because of the horse.'

'Horse, Kingsley? Oh, I see. You mean the vaulting-horse.'

'Sir, sir, *I* measured the horse,' shouted Sibling, normally a sensible little lad who gives no trouble. 'It's four foot three.'

'In its hocks?' asked some fool.

I quietened them with a frown and, after a little delay, wrote down a figure for the width of the gymnasium. 'Now then,' I said. 'To cover the floor of the gym with linoleum, which is sold in strips four feet wide at 10s. 11d a yard –'

'*Lino*, sir?' asked Notting.

'Wouldn't it be easier to wallpaper the cricket pitch?' suggested Mason.

I threw the chalk into a corner and went to my desk.

'So much for the new method in mathematics,' I said in a tone of voice there was no mistaking. 'You will now open your algebra books at page 153, Simultaneous Equations, Exercise 48.'

'Oh sir, why sir?' some of them cried. But of course I took no notice, and I distinctly heard one boy whisper 'I think he has eliminated "why?".'

He was quite right, whoever it was.

The Time-Bomb Affair

Apparently Matron has been putting it about that I was spearing fish in the hall at the masters' cottage yesterday evening. Anyone who knows me well will realize that I have better things to do with my time, and I should have ignored the whole thing but for the fact that these rumours sooner or later get round to the Headmaster and are best nipped in the bud. Once or twice, in my experience, he has taken a whimsical delight in deliberately misunderstanding some little incident that a word of explanation could easily put right. I was *not* wearing flippers, which in any case would be useless in an enamel washtub, and as for the spear which Matron claims that I held in my right hand – though I am at a loss to know how she could make out anything at all through the bottle-glass in the front door – this was an ordinary bread-knife, as I could have shown her on the spot had she not rushed away before I had time to get my shirt on or attempt any kind of explanation.

The fact is that Mrs Fitch, an old friend whom I met in Switzerland, had kindly sent me an alarm clock, which had been wound up, ill-advisedly as it turned out, before dispatch. I found the parcel awaiting me on my return to the cottage after Afternoon School, and carried it (not at that time, of course, knowing its contents) into Gilbert's room to borrow a pair of scissors. 'Aha!' he said, jumping up. 'A present from an admirer? Some little trifle from the Dunmow Fitch, A.J.?' This rather feeble joke (the lady concerned has never, so far as I am aware, lived in Essex) I should ordinarily have taken exception to, but Gilbert, who was by now pretending to scrutinize the postmark, suddenly changed expression and gave a startled cry. 'Good God!' he said. 'It's ticking'; and before I could stop him rushed into the kitchen and plunged my parcel into a bucket of water.

This extraordinary action he has since attempted to defend on the ground that one never knows and that a man in my position has many enemies. My personal opinion is that Gilbert reads too many novels and newspapers of a sensational kind, with the result that he is highly strung for a man of his age. But of course it is not easy to be angry with a man who, however mistaken, has acted with courage and presence of mind; and one has always to be on one's guard against being 'wise after the event' as the saying is. I am, I suppose, the last person in the world to be sent a time-bomb by parcel post, but then again it is to just such unlikely people, so I am told, that these infernal machines are addressed. All in all, it is not with Gilbert that I am inclined to pick a bone over this affair.

Be that as it may, there was my parcel in the water; nor, despite my remonstrances, would Gilbert allow me to withdraw it until the ticking had stopped. I therefore put my ear to the bucket and assured him, truthfully enough, that I could hear nothing. He was still dissatisfied, however – maintaining, absurdly enough, that it might not be possible to hear ticking through water. This argument went clean against all my training. Sound, as I told him, is *magnified* by water; and I adduced a number of instances by way of illustration, e.g. the need for absolute quiet when operating submarines in enemy waters, and the resonant ease (if a homely allusion may be forgiven me) with which braces etc, thrown carelessly over a bathroom radiator, can be heard downstairs. Finally, to prove my point, I thrust my left wrist, on which I wear a waterproofed watch, beneath the surface of the bucket and invited Gilbert to listen in his turn. He did so, and triumphantly declared that he could hear no ticking – which proved *his* point. However, on withdrawing my arm from the bucket I found that my waterproofed watch had stopped, so that we were no further on, in a way, though I shall certainly send a strongly worded note to my watchmaker.

I might have been wiser, looking back, to let the matter rest there. The Headmaster will certainly ask me, if the story comes to his ears, why I did not simply tell Gilbert to stop playing the fool and salvage my present before it was irretrievably ruined. The answer to that is that I did in fact remove the parcel from the bucket and lay it down on top of what proved to be a set of essays awaiting correction. But I confess that it's recovery no longer presented itself to my mind as a primary consideration. What now seemed to me of paramount importance – and if the Headmaster cares to call it stubbornness it will be news to me that to be stubborn in the pursuit of truth is a serious fault in a schoolmaster – what I was intent upon at this stage was to convince Gilbert of the audibility of sound through water. I accordingly cast about for a plan.

To plunge a succession of clocks and watches into the bucket was out of the question. For one thing, experience had shown that any timepiece so treated was likely to stop ticking at once; for another, we had no more working clocks or watches in the cottage, apart from the grandfather clock in the hall which is five feet high and not readily submersible. But it occurred to me that the necessary conditions would be fulfilled if the situation was reversed – in other words, if the *listener* were under water while the timepiece ticked against the side of the vessel containing him.

'Admirable!' Gilbert said, when I had outlined this idea. 'It is always advisable, when defending an untenable theory, to claim that its truth can be proved by an experiment which there is no possibility of carrying out.'

'I don't know so much about that,' I said, and after a momentary hesitation went into the scullery and brought out a sizeable enamel washtub. Gilbert's attitude, to tell the truth, had rather put me on my mettle. I am not a man to be deterred by difficulties when my good faith is called in question, so that I almost instinctively began to translate into action what had at first been no more than a half-jocular speculation.

'Here,' I said. 'Give me a hand with this table. We want to raise the tub until it is as near as possible touching the works of the grandfather clock.'

'Do you seriously intend –' he said, beginning to giggle in a rather childish way, 'You can't honestly –'

'Run the garden hose out here from the kitchen tap, my boy,' I told him briskly. 'You asked for it and you are going to get it, my lad,' I added under my breath. Fond as I am of my old colleague, who has been a staunch friend in many of life's ups and downs, there could be no harm in showing him that it does not pay to bandy arguments about sonic properties with a man who was studying them while he was still in his pram. While Gilbert was still in his pram, that is to say. At any rate, I thought with a quiet grin, it will teach him not to be too hasty with other people's parcels in future.

Well, in the end we had the tub filled, without very much help from Gilbert who wasted time with meaningless laughter and kept interjecting such remarks as 'Jump in the fire rather than be proved wrong' – of which, in the context, I could make nothing; the whole point of the experiment being that I should be proved *right*. Then, without any prompting from me, he ran off to his room and came back with his snorkel, a kind of breathing apparatus picked up at Hyères, with which he is a little over-inclined to show off in the swimming bath.

'What's the point of that?' I asked.

'It'll help you to listen in comfort,' he said. 'You don't want to burst your lungs waiting for the ticks.'

'I?' I laughed, unable to help seeing the comical side of the business. 'It is *you* who have to listen, not I. *I* need no convincing that sound is audible through water.'

To my astonishment, he flatly refused to play his part: declared that he had no intention of emulating Goldsmith's cat, and even talked a lot of nonsense about not depriving me of the full credit. 'This may go down in history as Wentworth's Law,' he said. 'It will be on a par with the

Michelson-Morley Experiment. After all, that proved nothing either.'

So there it was. In the face of such feeble timidity I should have been fully justified in chucking up the whole thing. Indeed, I was so angry that I nearly did so. But I frankly confess that I felt it my duty, quite apart from the intrinsic interest of the experiment, to teach young Gilbert a lesson. I at least am not afraid of a little cold water; and if it is wrong in an older man to show an example to a younger, that is a peccadillo to which I gladly plead guilty. I have little patience with namby-pambyism, as IIIA well know.

I therefore removed some of my upper garments without a word, took up a kneeling position on the table, and was adjusting the mouthpiece of the breathing-tube when my attention was distracted by a commotion on the further side of the front door and Gilbert, who had been drumming his heels on the floor in a rather silly pretended paroxysm of mirth, broke off to shout 'Golly! It's Matron!' Not unnaturally I lost my balance and, in attempting to regain it, caught hold of the side of the washtub, with results that have been as usual exaggerated. The plain bone-handled knife, characteristically mistaken by Matron for a spear, I had snatched up earlier to assist me in beating time with the clock against the side of the tub. It should hardly be necessary to explain that some such device was essential in order to prove to Gilbert that the sound of the clock's ticking was in fact audible when my head was under water. But experience has taught me that, here at Burgrove, it is necessary to explain *everything*.

I have some hope that, with Gilbert to substantiate my account of this not very serious little incident, the stupider rumours will soon be stilled. Time will show. Meanwhile I had almost forgotten that I have yet to write a letter of thanks to Mrs Fitch for her generous thought.

Farewell Talk

I have always doubted the wisdom of letting young boys perform in public. There is no harm, I mean to say, in little shows got up by the School *for* the School – singing and so on – as long as nobody else is there, apart from the School and the staff. It is a very different kettle of fish when parents are present and perhaps a visiting bishop as well, and everybody is embarrassed from start to finish. It should surely be possible to give the prizes away and get straight on with the Tea afterwards, without adding 'An Entertainment by the Boys of Burgrove', as if some kind of light relief were needed to follow the Headmaster's address. Light relief indeed!

I blame some of my colleagues, really. A man should be satisfied to teach English Literature or Music or whatever it may be without wanting to put his goods in the shop window at the end of term. The rest of us could be trusted to assume that he had done his best, particularly in the absence of visible proof of how poor that best appeared to be. Nothing makes my heart sink more abysmally than to see 'Violin Solo. B. Thornton' in the programme of events, unless it be 'An Impression of the Death of Sir John Moore. By the Lower Fourth'. Of the Exhibition of Drawings on brown paper in the gymnasium I prefer to say nothing. It has never been suggested, certainly not in my hearing at least, that I should line my IIIA boys up on the stage and let them factorize half-a-dozen algebraical expressions in unison, *or* that the parents would like to see some of their written work hung up in the corridors. But there you are. I have nothing against music and poetry and so on in their proper place. *Out* of their proper place they simply encourage showing off; and whether it is the boys who are showing off or the masters responsible for all this public tomfoolery, is not for me to say.

I did say something, as a matter of fact, when Gilbert and Raikes were in the Common Room, and was rather surprised at the upshot. From Raikes, naturally, I expected no support. He would have the whole School doing the hornpipe, with himself in shorts on the bosun's whistle, if he could have his way. But Gilbert has been long enough at the game, one would have thought, to learn more sense. It is possible to be over tolerant.

'I don't know, A.J.,' he said. 'Where's the harm if a fond mother likes to hear her little boy reciting "Friends, Romans, countrymen" with his hands behind his back and a look of boiled misery on his face? Don't be a killjoy.'

'Oh, Shakespeare,' I said. 'Shakespeare is all very well, but you are living in the past. We are more up-to-date nowadays. Remember the end of last term?'

I at any rate had not forgotten. In the old days one knew what to expect, more or less. If a boy got right through *The Wreck of the Hesperus* without a mistake, he was applauded; if he had to look over his shoulder at Miss Percival (or Miss Thwaites, who took over later on) for help, he got an extra clap for trying. Who is to know, with these modern absurdities, whether the boy has got it right or not – unless, of course, as happened last term, he gives the show away.

Now as I was young and easy under the apple boughs

Half the trouble with Betterton, R. B., is that he is a good deal too inclined to be easy under the apple boughs, or anywhere else for that matter. It is really too much that he should be clapped for it. I remembering thinking at the time that if he were a little less easy under Gilbert he would stand a better chance of getting into Malvern, but one has to keep one's thoughts to oneself on these occasions. So there we all sat, while the rigmarole went on.

And honoured among wagons I was prince of the apple towns.

God bless my soul! The boy is only twelve.

Later on, in what I thought an overlong poem by any standards, Betterton proclaimed that he was also honoured among foxes and pheasants, which was good news, I hope, for his parents after his half-term Report. It was as much as I could do to sit still, particularly with old General Garman in the audience, who is by no means as deaf as people think.

Under the new-made clouds and happy as the heart was long,
In the sun born over and over
I ran my heedless ways
My braces – No, *my wishes races – raced*, rather – *through the hay-high house*

Few of us would have been any the wiser if Betterton had gone straight on. However, the silly boy made a long pause at this point, shifted his feet about, and looked up at the ceiling – to which, as it happens, the Headmaster does *not* wish attention to be drawn. '*House hay*', he said at last; and stopped again.

The following ludicrous dialogue, as well as I recall it, then took place.

Miss Thwaites. House-high hay.
Betterton. Ho. I mean how high. No.
Miss Thwaites (*distinctly*). HOUSE-HIGH hay.
Betterton. Oh yes, of course. Heigh-ho house.
Miss Thwaites. HI. HAY-high, rather.
Betterton. I said that.
Miss Thwaites (*very pink*). Never mind. Go on from hay.
Betterton. Hay?
Miss Thwaites. House, then.
Betterton (*defiantly*). Hay. And nothing I cared at my skoo bligh trades . . .
Miss Thwaites(*now giggling openly*). Sky blue trades, boy.
Betterton. Oh damn.

If this sort of thing improves the reputation of the School, all I can say, as I told Gilbert when I reminded him of it, is that we are starting from a very low level indeed. Nothing of the kind could have happened if Miss Thwaites, or whoever was responsible, had had the gumption to stick to *Julius Caesar* or *Hamlet*. Or better still, as I began by saying, if there had been no 'Entertainment' at all.

'Well, well. You may be right,' Gilbert agreed, when I had had my say. 'As a matter of fact, we've been thinking that a bit of a change would be a good idea this term. I believe old Saunders is going to ask you to give a talk.'

'A talk!' I cried. 'I? This is the first I have heard of any such thing.'

'With slides, of course,' Gilbert added, picking up his gown. 'You could manage the projector all right, I imagine, Raikes?'

'Oh, yes,' Raikes said, rubbing his hands in an annoying way he has. 'Yes indeed. I can manage the projector all right.'

'And it isn't as if anyone of importance were coming this time,' Gilbert said over his shoulder, and went off whistling.

Anyone of importance! Does the silly fellow suppose I should be frightened of a few bishops and generals, deaf or not? I have talked to some pretty important people in my time, such as – well, all sorts, *and* on both sides of the Atlantic, which is more than he or Raikes could claim. I dare say, come to think of it, I could tell them all this and that about my visit to the States. It happens too that, though no photographer, I brought back with me a fair selection of 'transparencies' (to use the technical term) of the kind one can buy ready-made at places of interest over there. The White House, for instance, if I had been there. So, if I am asked, I have no doubt I can put together something that will be at least as much of an eye-opener, to put it no higher, as Thornton on the violin. One would not mind taking a little trouble, if it was to save the School from another houseful of hay from young Betterton.

We shall see. It may turn out to be just one of Gilbert's more tasteless jokes.

Well, it was no joke, after all. 'We'd be most grateful, if you would,' the Headmaster told me. 'And it will be a splendid send-off for you, my dear fellow.'

'Off – or up?' put in Gilbert, whose sense of humour at times verges on a IIIA level.

'I will do my best, of course, if you really wish it, Headmaster,' I replied. 'It will be just the staff and boys, I understand?'

'Just the staff and boys,' he repeated. 'We like to keep the best things to ourselves, eh Gilbert?'

Which was a very pleasant way of putting it, I thought, and made me quite determined to 'put on a good show', as we used to say in the Army.

I had no photographs of the ship to show them, only a very large menu card with about fifty different dishes on it, which could not of course be shown on the screen and in any case would have been hardly fair to the boys *or* staff after the supper we had just had. So I just talked to them for a bit, with the 'house lights' up (another technical phrase, this time a stage term I picked up from Megrim, or it may have been Miss Stephens, which goes to show how broadening my experiences of the last year or so have been). I told them about the colour of the Atlantic and so on, just as I put it down in my diary at the time, and how I missed the whale through being asleep, which went down very well. And when I came to the man bringing rope out of the dummy funnel they simply roared. 'It would be a fine thing,' I said on the spur of the moment, 'if one of your masters turned out to be a dummy!', and they made so much noise at this sally that in the end I had to call them to order by rapping on the floor with my stick or pointer.

'First slide, please, Mr Raikes,' I decided, to calm them, and as soon as the lights were down was beginning to tell them that the Empire State Building is over a thousand feet high when I happened to glance at the screen and was immediately obliged to break off.

'What on earth is that?' I demanded in astonishment.

'It looks very like King's College Chapel,' suggested the Headmaster mildly, and somebody at the back – Rawlinson, I think – called out 'I knew they had transhipped the old London Bridge, but this is *too* much.'

Raikes had no explanation of his extraordinary blunder, nor did I care to embarrass him further by stating that King's College had no business whatever to be included in my set of transparencies. So I simply said, quite quietly, 'Next, please,' and when the picture appeared on the screen refused, once again, to allow myself to be rattled, merely remarking smoothly 'When *I* saw the Empire State Building it was the other way up. But of course the New York skyline changes so rapidly these days – ah, thank you, there we are. The top of it' – and I indicated with my pointer the part I was talking about – 'is said to sway as much as thirty feet in a high wind.'

'Golly!' exclaimed one or two of the boys. And no wonder.

'Each way?' someone asked.

'Well naturally,' I replied, after a pause. 'When it sways one way, it has to sway back the opposite way; otherwise it would stay permanently bent, would it not?'

'What I meant was, does it sway fifteen feet from the vertical one way and fifteen the other, making thirty in all? Or does it do the full thirty in one swoop?'

'A very good point, Mr Gilbert,' I said, recognizing the voice despite the darkness, and I was considering my further reply when Raikes interposed with a suggestion that it would be better to keep questions until the end – 'or we may never reach it' he added, in what I dare say he believed to be an inaudible aside. Not being very sure of the answer to Gilbert's question, I stifled a momentary gust of annoyance and readily agreed with Raikes's proposal.

'By all means,' I said cheerily. 'Let us get on with the pictures, Mr Raikes. Even if they sway as much as 180 degrees from the vertical,' I could not resist adding, with a little dig at the upside-down Empire State. 'Next slide, please.'

It would be tedious to pursue the course of my little talk from start to finish. My plan was to tell them where I went and what I saw, and to this scheme I adhered, except when some picture came up in the wrong order, whereupon I would make the necessary deviation in my route, a departure of which my audience were no doubt unaware. Once or twice I could not quite remember where I went next, as anybody might, and I made no bones about it. I simply said I should omit the next bit, which I had forgotten, and they all cheered sympathetically. The boys particularly liked a photograph, given to me by a friendly American from, I think, Utah, of the far end of the Moffat Tunnel taken from about halfway or a bit more.

'It looks like the pinpoint of light when you switch off the telly,' some boy remarked, amid laughter. But I pointed out that the television spot grows smaller and disappears, whereas the end of the tunnel gets bigger all the time. 'Had you there, Mason,' I said, drawing a bow at not much of a venture.

'Not if it's the end you came in at,' he replied, thereby confirming my suspicions. However, I left it at that and pushed on to my next port of call, which turned out to be the Magazine at Williamsburg, owing to some muddle by Raikes. Rather a far cry from the Rockies, eh? But I am not easily put out of my stride, and passed it off with a joke about American hustle.

I had a surprise for them at the end. 'And now, boys,' I said, 'I conclude by showing you a place that, amid all the wonders I saw on this exciting adventure, was never far from my thoughts and, indeed, if you will forgive me for saying so, from my affections. Next slide, please.'

And there, to my distress, was that confounded King's College Chapel again, upside-down into the bargain.

'No, *no*, Raikes,' I cried. 'The *last* slide.'

'Do you mean the one we've just had?' he asked. 'Or –

oh, I see. All right, all right, wait a minute.'

Good grief! Even Betterton, R.B., would have done better – no pun intended!

After a good deal of shuffling about, and some muffled language which I hope the boys could not catch, he found what I wanted: a view of Burgrove School taken from the south-east specially for me by Miss Thwaites, who dabbles in that kind of thing.

'I'm afraid rather a lot of light has got in,' I heard her say, to which I riposted 'More than I have managed to get into my IIIA Set, I fear' – but I doubt whether anyone heard me, owing to the volume of applause as I laid aside my pointer.

As soon as the house lights were switched on the Headmaster got to his feet and spoke very kindly about my talk and – well, about my long service to the School. 'I am sure Mr Wentworth must be tired,' he ended, 'and as time is getting on we must excuse him the promised Question Time. Three cheers for Arthur Wentworth, doyen of Burgrove!'

I was not at all tired, as it happens, but of course one does not contradict one's Headmaster, or certainly not in the presence of the boys. Besides, the cheering rather put an end to things, and when they all sang 'For he's a jolly good fellow' I could not have said another word, even if asked. My eyes were quite wet, I am not ashamed to say, and I might have fallen rather heavily as I stepped, or stumbled, from the dais, had not Raikes sprung adroitly to my aid. He is a good chap, really, and one has no right, I suppose, to expect athleticism *and* intelligence.

Supper at Elm Cottage

On the last morning, after most of the boys had already left for home, I wandered alone about the School grounds and buildings thinking long thoughts – by no means the perquisite of youth, as the poet would have it. There it all was, my second home, indeed you might say my only home in a sense for so many, many years. The cricket pavvy, still in need of a coat of paint as it was when I came back from the War; the old roller by the gym that we trundled about so absurdly when the Inspectors visited us, not so very long ago that, though; the path to Marling Woods, where the boy Phillips got himself into such a pickle in a culvert, oh a quarter of a century ago or more it must have been; and the Museum! What a fuss! I still think young Malcolm should have been caned for it – 'and there an end', as another poet rightly says. Everything full of memories, some to make me chuckle, some with more sombre undertones. The swimming pool for some reason – I forget the incident – put me in mind of that man Faggott, and I hurried indoors again for a last look at my old classroom, not forgetting to take a peep on my way into the cupboard outside Common Room, where I thought I had left my umbrella that time old Saunders and Gilbert behaved so childishly.

When I opened the door into IIIA, whom should I see ferreting about in his desk but young Mason of all people.

'Not gone yet then?' I asked him.

'No, sir. My father can't get here much before three, unfortunately.'

'Oh, I see,' I said. 'Still, the time will soon go.'

Not knowing what else to say, I picked up a piece of chalk and began to flip it up and down, as I used to do when momentarily at a loss over some problem. A sudden desire came over me to write some kind of farewell message on the board, though of course it would have been wiped off by the cleaners long before the boys returned, and in any case I was saved from such uncharacteristic folly when Mason looked up from his desk and said, rather shyly, 'I say, sir. I'm sorry if I've been rather, well, a bit tiresome at times, sir.'

'I've known worse,' I said gruffly, and added, before I could stop myself, 'I shall be sorry to miss your father. My cab will be here in half-an-hour.'

Mason just grinned at me, and I dare say my own mouth twitched a bit at the corners. 'It's been fun, sir, hasn't it, all the same?' he said.

'It has indeed, young fellow,' I agreed. 'It has indeed.' And on a sudden impulse I went across and shook him by the hand.

'Good luck!' I said. 'Think of me sometimes.' Then I put the chalk back where it belonged and went quickly away.

It was almost half-past six when I reached my cottage, and found to my surprise a bright fire burning in the grate. Myra Fitch had, of course, very properly moved out a few days before my return, and Mrs Bretton leaves directly she has washed up the lunch, even had there been any lunch to clear up, which of course on that day there was not. Who could have been in, I wondered? Still, there it was, a very cheering sight on what had been in many ways a rather saddening day.

I busied myself unpacking and generally settling in, and I very soon noticed that my blue bedroom curtains with the white sailing ships on them, which I chose myself, had been taken down and orange ones with zig-zags, very modern I dare say, put up in their place. This without reference to me, which I thought strange, to say the least. There was also something unfamiliar about the bathroom, and when I came downstairs again I was vexed to find that the coal-scuttle had been moved to the other side of the fireplace, not to mention a ridiculous thing like a tea-cosy placed over the telephone. I suppose, when one let's one's house, no matter to whom, there are bound to be drawbacks, but I was tired and not in a mood for fripperies. A cup of tea and a boiled egg, if I could find such a thing, might put me in a more equable frame of mind.

First, though, I must read the note that Mrs Fitch, with whose handwriting I am familiar, had left upon my desk. Just a single sheet of paper, with her cheque for the last month's rent pinned to it, and nothing more in the way of apology or explanation for what she had been up to in my absence than a brief 'I hope you will approve of the small changes I have ventured to make in your charming home.' All very well, but really! However, it was the last few lines that properly took my breath away.

'I am sure you will be glad to know,' she wrote, 'that I am soon to be married again. Sidney Megrim, an old friend of yours I believe, has asked me to be his wife – all rather sudden, you may think, but that is how these things happen – and I know we shall be very happy together. I am delighted that Fenport is to be my home, and it is nice to think that we shall be able to see quite a lot of you. I hope you think so too!'

And that, with the addition of the usual 'Forgive this hurried scrawl. I must rush' – so typical of a woman – was that. *Megrim*! Altogether too offhand a feller-me-lad, in my opinion, *and* can't even stop his dog fouling the footpaths, which is not much of a recommendation for married life, or so I should have thought. It is not too much to say that I felt a bit flabbergasted.

I paced about the room, a prey to very mixed emotions. On the one hand, there had been a time when I – but there is no need to go into that now. On the other, I must confess to a certain sense of relief, ungallant though it may sound, particularly when my eye was caught again by that thing on the telephone. 'A narrow squeak, eh, Wentworth,' I found myself saying, and I could not resist a quiet chuckle when I thought what a smack in the eye this would be for my nosey old colleagues, should they come to hear of it.

I was musing in this way, with half my mind on that contemplated cup of tea, when there was a knock on the door and, to my amazement, who should appear but Miss Stephens. 'Why, what an unexpected pleasure!' I cried, and I meant it, too.

'Come in, come in, come in, Miss Stephens,' I said warmly, plumping up the cushion on my best armchair, which, as I should have mentioned before, seemed to have become a great deal more garish – the cushion, I mean, not of course the chair – since I last saw it. 'Sit you down by the fire. This is indeed –'

'Oh, Mr Wentworth,' she said, 'I really ought not to come bursting in on you like this, but I wanted to be sure you were comfortable and had everything you needed. . . .'

She was wearing a fur tippet, if that is what it is called, so becoming on a woman I always think, and a jaunty little red beret on the side of her head, and altogether looked quite a picture. She was carrying a largish basket, too, which I could not help noticing, as she set it down beside her chair, seemed to contain a cauliflower and other comestibles.

'I bet you have practically nothing to eat in the house,' she said, following the direction of my glance. 'So I wondered whether you would allow me just to whip you up something for supper. Do you like cauliflower cheese?'

'Allow you, Miss Stephens, allow you? I should jolly well think so, if you can really be –. Only on one condition,' I added, raising an admonitory forefinger, 'and that is that you have brought provisions for two.'

'Oh, I could hardly – I mean there are only the two of us, if you see what I mean.'

'I have a bottle of Burgundy under the stairs,' I mentioned casually. 'And as to the proprieties, we theatrical people are not expected to care about *them*.' This was a joking allusion to the play in which we both took part some months ago. I was beginning to feel quite light-hearted, having someone to talk to instead of the lonely evening I had been rather dreading.

'Burgundy!' she cried, with a bright smile. 'Now that I cannot resist.'

'Burgundy it shall be,' I replied, rubbing my hands before the fire (which I shrewdly suspected Miss Stephens, who of course held the key of my cottage, of having herself kindled for me). 'Assuming, that is,' I added, as if to myself, 'that the bottle has not been included among the other alterations that Mrs Myra Fitch, to give her her present title, has seen fit to make in my humble abode.'

She gave me a look that I could not quite fathom. 'I see,' said after a pause, glancing in her turn at the letter which I still, rather clumsily, held in my hand, 'I see that you have heard about – about Myra. I hope it has not come as too much of a shock.'

'Oh that,' I assured her. 'Oh yes, yes, I have heard about that. One can only trust that Sidney Megrim shares her somewhat peculiar tastes in, ah, in upholstery and so forth. Not,' I concluded, with perhaps a touch of acidity, 'that he is likely to be consulted in the matter.'

'That's naughty,' Miss Stephens said, and positively burst out laughing. 'What fun it all is!' Though just what she meant by the latter remark I was at a loss to know – much as I was inclined to agree, nonetheless.

It was pleasant to lie back in my chair, listening to the clatter of pots and pans as Miss Stephens busied herself in my kitchen; and a very good meal we made of it, on a little occasional table by the fire, 'just to be cosy', as my kindly companion said. Afterwards we chatted about this and that, and at her insistence I told her all about my American adventures, so that it was quite late when Miss Stephens sprang to her feet crying 'Good heavens, I must fly! My reputation, such as it is, will be in ruins.'

'Everyone knows that you are perfectly safe with *me*,' I said reassuringly, and once again she gave me a rather baffling look. 'Can you be sure of that, Mr Wentworth?' she asked me; to which I made no reply, not being very sure of anything, to tell the truth, except that I had thoroughly enjoyed the evening.

Miss Stephens protested, though not very strongly, at my determination to see her safely home, and we walked along together very companionably despite a slight drizzle. 'Mr Wentworth,' she suddenly broke out, after we had been silent for a while, 'I hope you don't think I have been very tiresome and impertinent in some of the things – I mean what I was saying to you in Mellish's that day, oh, and other times. It was very silly of me. I don't know why. . . .'

'My dear young lady,' I exclaimed, coming to a halt. 'You really must not think me such a touchy old fuddy-duddy as all that. You may say whatever you like to me. I have the highest – why only this morning one of my boys was apologizing in case I might have been hurt by his – but that is neither here nor there. I am afraid I hardly know what I am saying. It is just that, after all these years, Miss Stephens – oh, botheration! I should very much like, if I had your permission, and if I knew your Christian name – which I *don't*,' I ended lamely and sounding, I fear, a little huffy in my confusion.

'My name is Felicity,' she told me rather breathlessly, for I had walked on with a quickened stride after my sadly bungled appeal. 'You may not like it, but I'm afraid it is too late to change it now.'

'It may be too late to change your first name,' I was surprised to hear myself saying, 'but it is by no means too late – that is to say, I think Felicity is a very nice name indeed. A very nice name.' Steady on, old chap, I thought to myself. You have no right, no right at all.

Miss Stephens, or Felicity rather, as I now have permission to call her, turned a little pink, or so I thought, though the street lighting in Fenport leaves a great deal to be desired, and quietly slipped her arm through mine. 'I shall call you Jimmy, if I may,' she said. 'I know *your* names, you see.'

Jimmy! Nobody has called me anything but 'A.J.' and 'Wentworth, old boy' for as long as I can remember.

Well, we were at her house soon after that, and she stood on the step for a moment while I racked my brains for something to say. My mind was in a bit of a whirl, if all the truth were known.

'You have been extremely kind,' I got out at last, 'extremely kind and friendly to a rather lonely and, until you came, a rather sad old fellow. Might I, Miss – that is to say, may I call to say thank you, Felicity, for being so good to me? Tomorrow, perhaps?'

'Will this do for an answer?' she asked. Then she leant forwards, put her two gloved hands on my rain-soaked shoulders, and gave me the lightest kiss just above my right eyebrow.

Such a thing had not happened to me before in all my life.

A Fragment from *The Fenport Chronicle*

. . . with matching accessories.

Among the guests at St Martin's Church and afterwards at the reception in St Mark's Hall were: Colonel and Mrs Ripley, Commander and Mrs Mason, with their elder son Geoffrey, Mr and Mrs Sidney Megrim, Major Thorpe, Mr and Mrs Odding, Miss Edge, Miss Thwaites, Mr Rawlinson, Mr Raikes, Mr and Mrs Wheeler, Mr Ernie Craddock representing the Fenport Football Club, Mrs Bretton, Miss Coombes. Greetings telegrams included several from the groom's friends in the United States.

Proposing the health of the happy couple, the Revd Gregory Saunders, headmaster of Mr Wentworth's old school, who assisted the Revd Somers at the service, animadverted on the groom's remarkable gifts as a teacher, saying he would be greatly missed, but that Burgrove's loss was Fenport's gain. In a humorous vein he went on to say that he understood that the couple had first met through the local Dramatic Society and he felt sure that the bride would see to it that her husband did not fluff his marriage lines. Mr Wentworth replied at length with scholarly wit, thanking all his good friends in both continents for their help and good wishes.

Mr Charles Gilbert, best man, declined to reveal the honeymoon destination. 'Not that it would matter if I did,' he told our reporter, 'because, if Mr Wentworth has anything to do with it, he will almost certainly finish up somewhere else.'

The last sentence in this report has been underlined in ink and marginally annotated, in a familiar hand, 'Fiddle-de-dee!'

On the following pages are details of Arrow books that will be of interest.

A. J. WENTWORTH, BA

H. F. Ellis

'One of the funniest books ever . . . it deserves to follow *The Henry Root Letters* to the top of the bestsellers' *Sunday Express*

There is chalk in his fingernails and paper darts fill the air as A. J. Wentworth, BA, mathematics master at Burgrove Preparatory School, unwittingly opens the doors that lead not to knowledge but to chaos and confusion. Here are his collected papers in which you can at last discover the truth about the fishing incident in the boot room, the real story about the theft of the headmaster's potted plant, and even the answer to the sensitive question of whether or not Mr Wentworth was trying to have carnal knowledge of matron on that one, memorable occasion.

'I did indeed laugh aloud till I cried' *Graham Lord, Sunday Express*

'A book of such hilarious nature that I had to give up reading it in public as my shrieks were causing both surprise and annoyance to those present' *Arthur Marshall, New Statesman*

'Few books have made me laugh out loud quite so often' *Christopher Matthew, Evening Standard*

£1.25

CAROLINE R

David Lancaster

What would it take to topple the British throne? Revolution? Bankruptcy? Political chaos? Or a beautiful and rebellious young Queen?

It was a storybook romance come true. He was the popular young King who had searched so long for love. She was the striking young heiress who seemed born to be made a queen. The whole world watched their wedding, caught up in their love – it seemed a time for happy endings . . .

But more depends on a royal marriage than personal happiness. In a world of protocol and form, feelings are a luxury, desires a danger – what chance has love against the demands of State?

'Fascinating' *Daily Telegraph*

£1.50